Get Your Coventry Romances Home Subscription NOW

And Get These 4 Best-Selling Novels *FREE*:

LACEY
by Claudette Williams

THE ROMANTIC WIDOW
by Mollie Chappell

HELENE
by Leonora Blythe

THE HEARTBREAK TRIANGLE
by Nora Hampton

A Home Subscription! It's the easiest and most convenient way to get every one of the exciting Coventry Romance Novels! ...And you get 4 of them FREE!

You pay nothing extra for this convenience; there are no additional charges...you don't even pay for postage! Fill out and send us the handy coupon now, and we'll send you 4 exciting Coventry Romance novels absolutely FREE!

SEND NO MONEY, GET THESE
FOUR BOOKS FREE!

C0181

MAIL THIS COUPON TODAY TO:
**COVENTRY HOME SUBSCRIPTION SERVICE
6 COMMERCIAL STREET
HICKSVILLE, NEW YORK 11801**

YES, please start a Coventry Romance Home Subscription in my name, and send me FREE and without obligation to buy, my 4 Coventry Romances If you do not hear from me after I have examined my 4 FREE books, please send me the 6 new Coventry Romances each month as soon as they come off the presses. I understand that I will be billed only $10.50 for all 6 books There are no shipping and handling nor any other hidden charges. There is no minimum number of monthly purchases that I have to make In fact, I can cancel my subscription at any time The first 4 FREE books are mine to keep as a gift, even if I do not buy any additional books

For added convenience, your monthly subscription may be charged automatically to your credit card

☐ Master Charge   ☐ Visa

Credit Card #_____

Expiration Date_____

Name_____

Address_____
  Please Print

City_____State_____Zip_____

Signature_____

☐ Bill Me Direct Each Month

This offer expires March 31, 1981. Prices subject to change without notice Publisher reserves the right to substitute alternate FREE books. Sales tax collected where required by law. Offer valid for new members only.

CHASTITY'S PRIZE

Darrell Husted

FAWCETT COVENTRY • NEW YORK

For Bill Gilbertson

CHASTITY'S PRIZE

Published by Fawcett Coventry Books, a unit of CBS Publications, the Consumer Publishing Division of CBS Inc.

Copyright © 1980 by Darrell Husted

All Rights Reserved

ISBN: 0-449-50158-2

Printed in the United States of America

First Fawcett Coventry printing: January 1981

10 9 8 7 6 5 4 3 2 1

Chapter One

Though Chastity Dalrymple was not a particularly adaptable person, she was sufficiently flexible to have gotten through her twenty-seven years with minimum conflict. She had strong opinions, it was true, but she was also gifted with tact and a basic good nature that kept them within reasonable bounds. She might believe, for example, that her sisters were spoiling their children, and she might even point this out to them, but at the same time she would temper her judgment by helping with the dressing, feeding and amusement of these same flawed offspring. She was capable of making tart observations about those who wandered into her vicinity, but was always careful to gauge the impact of her tongue, and rarely ever inflicted more than a sting on the objects of her displeasure. At Grangeford, the estate in Kent where she was raised, she had created a halo of authority and credibility about herself that almost no one, not even her father, challenged anymore.

But now she was in London, and this halo had not traveled well. The principal cause of its dissipation was her Aunt Isabelle, the Dowager Duchess of Trentower. This lady—the half-sister of her father, seventy-two years old, and straight and thin as a stick—had reached a period of her life in which she felt she could dispense with the inessential furbelows of social intercourse. Consequently she rarely ever refined her impulses, which usually arose to the detriment of whomsoever happened to fall under her view. For the past three months Chastity had been the object of her unrelenting scrutiny.

The meeting between aunt and niece had not begun auspiciously. "So you've come to London to find a husband, I suppose," said Lady Trentower as Chastity stepped into her foyer after the tiring trip from Grangeford. "And high time too, I should say. You're how old? Twenty-seven, is it? A little long in the tooth, but I daresay some bachelor can be flushed. Your dowry, after all, is not inconsiderable."

The situation, of course, was much more complex than that—Chastity was, in a sense, fleeing an offer of marriage in Kent—yet if one did not put too fine a point on the matter her aunt's remark was essentially correct, and this made it all the more galling.

Chastity had responded ineptly. "No, ma'am," she had said, "I have come to London simply to broaden my experience and to see the sights of the city."

"Indeed," Lady Trentower had replied, incredulity stamped on her heavily painted face. She made no effort to disguise her annoyance at the patent falsehood.

Chastity would have been better off to have stated her position as honestly as she could. She was, however, incapable of unraveling the twisted skein of her situation in the best of circumstances, and certainly was not about to undertake such a task on the defensive. So she had resorted to a glacial formality for protection, while her aunt continued, almost gleefully, to disdain any word or gesture that would becloud the relationship with graciousness.

In spite of their constant, though muted, hostility to each other, Lady Trentower had been remarkably successful in leading her niece to the right places at the right time. Even though the season had not begun—it was now March—Chastity had already attracted a respectable amount of attention from several worthy gentlemen, and had found particular favor with one, Charles Techett.

"He would not be a bad catch," mused Lady Trentower, after his second visit. "Though he's a widower, he is of good family and his late wife left him upwards of twenty thousand pounds. The income from that, along with your dowry, will do very nicely. You have no objections to a widower, I presume?"

Chastity had replied shortly that she had none. She might have added, had she felt more affable toward her aunt, that she particularly had no objections when the widower was a man of thirty-three years, lean, with black eyes, fair skin and an elegance of manner and speech. Furthermore, she had known of the existence of Charles Techett for eleven years, and he had in a disembodied way become the symbol of all the romance that was lacking at Grangeford. She did not tell her aunt that, either.

Lady Trentower had continued, "He is the youngest son of Lord and Lady Quarles—at least that is the official attitude toward his parentage.

Nearly everyone is aware that in all likelihood his real father was your late uncle, William." Chastity had known that, also, although she merely nodded as though the information were unworthy of more than passing attention. Her apparent sophistication riled her aunt. "What is more," Lady Trentower had persisted rather disagreeably, "Charles Techett was the lover of Evelyn de Brey before she became your late uncle's wife." She gave this news with triumphant anticipation. She was disappointed again, for Chastity merely nodded politely and murmured, "How interesting," in the tone of voice one uses when replying to a not very interesting tidbit of gossip.

For in fact, the whole drama of her uncle's marriage to his godson's (or son's, according to gossip) mistress had begun at Grangeford under the fascinated eyes of Chastity and her sisters, Faith and Hope. They had watched spellbound as their uncle, Lord Grasset, had arrived with the most glittering entourage they had ever seen, and had gasped when he had handed Evelyn de Brey down from his coach. Her beauty was so piercing it banished jealousy or envy; Lord Grasset had remarked to her father that Evelyn was, in all likelihood, the most beautiful woman of her era. Certainly no one at Grangeford disputed the judgment. Little by little the strange relationship between Lord Grasset and Evelyn de Brey came to light. She had been the mistress of Lord Grasset's godson, Charles Techett, who was the youngest son of Lord and Lady Quarles (at least officially) and who had absolutely no fortune of his own; in order to survive he would have to marry money. His mother had sought out the Honorable Letitia

Bowen and her inheritance of twenty thousand pounds. Arrangements were made for the young people to meet, but, understandably, before her family would agree to discussing the matter they insisted that Charles break with his mistress. This was no simple matter, for Charles and Evelyn, it appeared, truly loved each other. She had been raised as a street singer, and had been saved from the sordid fate usually accorded such creatures only by a series of liaisons with wealthy and concupiscent gentlemen, beginning when she was twelve years old. Charles had taken her from this milieu and had begun to educate her. He was a practical and realistic young man, and he knew the affair could not last. At the same time, he was loathe to toss Evelyn back into the cesspool from which he had saved her. It even seemed to those who knew him that he might not be willing to give her up at all. That this was a real possibility became apparent when he finally delivered an ultimatum to his godfather: He would only send Evelyn away provided Lord Grasset would take her under his protection.

Lord Grasset had been understandably nonplussed at this singular stipulation. He had met Evelyn de Brey while she was living with Charles Techett, and had found her enchanting; but he was at the time a gentleman of sixty some-odd years, a widower, wealthy, and one of the most accomplished members of the Royal Society. To take on a mistress of Evelyn's dazzling splendor did not suit him at all. He demurred. Charles was adamant. If his godfather would not take direct responsibility for the girl then he, Charles, would not give her up. And that was that. Finally, in order to smooth the way for the negotiations with the Honorable Letitia Bowen's family, Lord Grasset agreed to a trial liaison. Evelyn was not informed of what had taken place; all she knew was that she had been separated for some reason from the man she loved. It was at this juncture that Lord Grasset gathered her up along with clothes enough for a royal princess, and declared they were going to tour Russia. Their first stop was at Grangeford, where they passed four days, and where Lord Grasset announced that he would marry Evelyn de Brey at sea on the way to Saint Petersburg.

The declaration had quite astounded the little group at Grangeford, all the more so since it was apparent to everyone who saw her that Evelyn de Brey was suffering from a broken heart at the loss of Charles. She had even tried to send him a letter, which had been intercepted by their neighbor's son who had been smitten by her (and who had since become the husband of Chastity's sister, Hope). All to no avail. Lord Grasset and Evelyn de Brey had departed together in a cloud of golden dust that had colored Chastity's life ever since. Of all the spectators of the drama that had taken place at Grangeford, Chastity was the only one who was deeply marked. Her sisters had accomplished humdrum but sensible marriages to the neighboring squire's sons. Chastity had berated them for not withholding themselves for something more exciting. She discouraged advances made by local swains, and there were not that many swains in the neighborhood, because she carried in her heart the certitude that she was intended for a romance as grand, as poignant, as all-encompassing as that experienced by the tragic Evelyn de Brey and Charles Techett—two star-crossed lovers who had been betrayed by circumstances into forgoing each other.

The images of the exquisite Evelyn and the romantic Charles had shimmered in her mind's eye for so many years that they had made reality tawdry. As she grew older, and as events and people continued to fall short of the standards set by this legendary couple, she became tart and even, on occasion, somewhat captious. She had never learned to forgive her relatives and acquaintances for not attempting to achieve the heights, and depths, of grand passions, for avoiding headlong dashes toward emotional abysses, or for sidestepping eternal commitments.

In spite of her predilection for the more operatic aspects of human behavior, Chastity was essentially a sensible girl; her background, breeding and surroundings accounted for that. Her yearning for romance was leavened by a cool analytic assessment of the facts. Consequently she never allowed herself to fall into the silly sighing, swooning poses of some of her less intelligent contemporaries. She stopped at analyzing her circumstances with objectivity and finding them lacking.

Since her basic good sense was garnished by an attractive face and figure, and by a more than decent dowry, she had been the object of several matrimonial campaigns. She had not been impressed by any of them. Or at least, she had not been sufficiently interested to encourage any of the men who had offered themselves.

Then Joseph Brockton hove into view. He began his pursuit in much the same way the others had—by visits, little gifts of game with respectful requests to be remembered to Miss Dalrymple, long and polite conversations with Mr. Dalrymple. Chastity wryly recognized all the signs of another courtship. Mr. Brockton was not unprepossessing, and he had recently acquired Harrowgate, a prosperous estate that was a scant twenty miles from Grangeford. He was in his late thirties, tall, a little stout, though not fat, his face a more dusky hue than was usually to be found in the temperate climate of Kent. The latter was accounted for by the fact that he had spent almost a dozen years in India with the East India Company where he had made a respectable amount of money, enough to buy Harrowgate, which did not go cheaply, and then have some left over. He came from a Cornwall family that was well-regarded, though not noble; his antecedents, however, were solid.

He had, indisputably, all the hallmarks of an acceptable husband as the world measures such matters. Unfortunately, as Chastity discovered early in their acquaintance, he lacked dash. When she first saw him, and heard that he had passed a dozen or so years in a remote and exotic climate, she assumed that he must be teeming with accounts of rebellion and mysterious customs. Not at all. He had passed his time, not on the backs of swaying elephants, nor hacking his way through perilous jungles, but rather at a desk in Calcutta. He had gained his interesting color, apparently, simply by traveling from his residence to his office and back again each day. "It is very hot in Calcutta, ma'am," was one of the insights he lay at Chastity's feet. She found it wanting.

It was not long before she accorded him the

same faintly amused condescension that had been the prelude to so many other polite dismissals. Her sisters watched with dismay as all the signs began to surface once more. She was then twenty-six years old. Her sisters had been married when they were eighteen and seventeen years old, and had settled comfortably into matronhood. They had been happy, and they could not understand why Chastity would not embrace the same felicity when it was offered her. They feared that her time was running short; after Mr. Brockton, it seemed unlikely there would be many others, if any at all.

This was a fear that Chastity shared, though she did not express it, nor allow it to be suspected by those near her. But in truth she wanted a husband and family. What else was there for her, after all? The alternative—to be a maiden daughter living out her years at Grangeford waiting on her father—was dismal indeed, even though the property was delightful and her parent congenial. Mr. Dalrymple was not, if truth be told, particularly interested in the outcome of the situation; he passed the greater part of his time in his library reading the ancients, and prided himself on his lack of attachment to worldly concerns, of which he considered his daughter among the least. If she stayed at Grangeford, that was fine with him, for she presented no difficulties, and if she married that was fine also. There was, in short, no pressure upon Chastity to take a spouse—but on the other hand she really had little choice but to do so. She truly wanted a husband, but she could not bear to lower her standards by accepting any of those who had presented themselves for the honor. It was, consequently, with a genuine sigh of regret that she began to ease Mr. Brockton toward the exit.

Mr. Brockton, however, proved more obdurate than his predecessors, and ignored the signs that were there for all to see. Though his invitations were refused and his pheasants not complimented; though his little sallies were greeted with unamused composure and his hints of ardor were received with stony-faced lack of acknowledgment; though all of these conditions prevailed, Mr. Brockton persisted. The man simply would not stay away. Not only did he lack dash, Chastity decided, he had a hide as thick as a cow's.

With increasing distress Chastity watched Mr. Brockton's arrivals for his twice, sometimes thrice, weekly visits. He would come galloping down the drive at Grangeford, and she had to admit that he sat his horse beautifully, and dismount like a cautious Lochinvar and rush up the stairs with all the enthusiasm of one who is fondly expected. She had done everything but slam the door in his face, and was at a loss as to how she could convey her displeasure at his obstinance.

What made the matter more delicate was that Mr. Brockton was not an obviously unacceptable suitor. In addition to the merits of income and family mentioned above, he was reasonably well-informed about political affairs, had done some reading, and enjoyed music when exposed to it. Had he been ostentatiously boorish or ignorant, or even unpolished, she might have had the support of her sisters, both of whom lived on the neighboring estate, in getting rid of him. But since all he lacked was dash, and since in Chastity's opinion this quality was equally lacking in her sisters' spouses, no one but she could fault the man. Everyone, including Chastity, agreed he was "a nice man."

In the midst of this dilemma came word that Lord Grasset, Mr. Dalrymple's half-brother, the husband of the exquisite Evelyn, had died in Russia where he and his wife had lived for the past ten years.

At Grangeford Lord and Lady Grasset had been all but forgotten by everyone but Chastity, nor were they often mentioned in London anymore. Lord Grasset had remained more or less in view because of the contributions he continued to make to the Royal Society (his paper on the fauna to be found in the steppes was judged every bit as excellent as his earlier work on the eruption of Vesuvius—and after that paper he had been proclaimed the foremost British authority on volcanoes). But no one talked any longer of the scandal that had ensued when it was learned that the sixty-odd-year-old baron had departed for Russia with his godson's twenty-year-old mistress and had been married at sea. The immense distance separating the strange couple from their homeland had vitiated their value as gossip.

When Chastity heard the news of her uncle's death her first thoughts were for the widow. She wondered how Evelyn was managing, alone in a barbaric country, for that is how Chastity imagined Russia in spite of that nation's recent invaluable aid in defeating Napoleon. As she recalled the slender young woman with the enormous black eyes leaning on the arm of Lord Grasset, quite literally standing under his protection, her heart expanded with sympathy at her plight. She had wanted to send a letter immediately, inviting the widow to Grangeford where she could mourn, if she were so inclined, or at least recuperate from the strain of her husband's death. But she had no idea where in the vast land Lady Grasset was to be found. The news had come to them from Lady Trentower, who had decided to inform her half-brother of the loss several weeks after she had learned of it herself.

This casual manner of imparting family news was typical of the relationship between Mr. Dalrymple and his half-sister. None of the three children of Andrew Dalrymple, the first Baron of Grasset had been close; by his first wife he had spawned William (later the second Baron Grasset, and Chastity's uncle) and Isabelle; after his first wife died, he married again and spawned Alfred, Chastity's father. None of the three siblings took any pains to keep in touch, but rather went their own ways. So Isabelle's letter, written almost as an afterthought, did not offend Mr. Dalrymple by its lateness and skimpiness of detail. He had not heard directly from either his brother or sister for years, nor they from him, so the demise of one of them was actually of minor interest to him.

"Dear, dear," he said absently at breakfast, the morning he received the letter. "Your uncle's dead."

Chastity had experienced a curious start, an involuntary intake of breath, as she asked, "Is that letter, then, from Evelyn?"

Mr. Dalrymple looked up, confused, as if he were trying to remember who Evelyn was. Then he said, "No, no, my dear, it's from Isabelle. In

London," he added, to make certain there would be no confusion.

"When did he die?" asked Chastity.

"Hmm. She doesn't say," replied Mr. Dalrymple, studying the brief note as though to find the answer somewhere between the lines. "I suppose some time ago."

"And Evelyn? Is she returning to England?"

"Ahh," said Mr. Dalrymple, again turning to the note, "Isabelle makes no mention whatsoever of Lady Grasset." He looked at his daughter blandly. "An oversight, I presume. Your Aunt Isabelle is not a great letter writer, at least, not to me."

Chastity thought the sentiment erred on the side of understatement.

Lady Trentower's letter, abbreviated though it was, did serve to renew, albeit fitfully, a correspondence between her and Mr. Dalrymple. He replied with appropriate condolences and a request for enlightenment. Lady Trentower, after an interval, supplied further information: Lord Grasset had been buried in Saint Petersburg at the request of his widow; what that widow's further plans were she could not say. The tone of the letter implied that, furthermore, the disposition of Evelyn, Lady Grasset, was the very least of her interests. Mr. Dalrymple had responded politely, and there the correspondence might have ended, but for Mr. Joseph Brockton.

For with the emergence of her aunt, Chastity saw a way of escaping Mr. Brockton's persistent attentions. She suggested to her parent that she should like to pay a visit to London, where she had never been. Mr. Dalrymple found the desire singular, even somewhat eccentric, but it was all the same to him if his youngest daughter wished to undertake the hardship of a two or three day voyage to the capital. It was a very simple matter to arrange. Mr. Dalrymple wrote to tell Isabelle of his daughter's desire and that woman had replied simply that her niece should come. It was all settled before Chastity quite realized just what she had been committed to.

It was after the plans had been made that Chastity was forced to confront her own motives. She had to admit that she was not only fleeing Mr. Brockton's attentions; she was also embracing the possibilities that the richest and most powerful city in the world offered. She was chasing, in other words, romance. The realization brought a blush to her face, for it was an admission that she wanted to be married just as badly as any other young woman in her situation. In fact, her desire for a husband was probably stronger because she had so far exceeded prime marriageable age; this detail added real challenge to the situation. At the same time she did not want just any husband, but one who could live up to her ideal—vague though that criterion might be. To complicate matters, no one, absolutely no one, should be aware of her goal.

Lady Trentower, however, had cut through her defenses with her initial tactless, curt, and all too accurate observation that Chastity had come to London for a husband. The remark reduced Chastity's situation to its barest bones, surely a cruel and crude method of dealing with any circumstance, and had made the younger woman irrevocably wary of the older one.

The two women had settled into a state of polite enmity almost from Chastity's first day in London. They disagreed about nearly everything, but always in most civil terms. Their restraint, however, was tested on this March morning, for Lady Trentower had just received news that offended her and that would, she was certain, offend any right thinking person.

"Imagine that," she said contemptuously, waving a letter in the air. "The woman wishes me to receive her."

Chastity barely lifted her head from the perusal of her own correspondence—a letter from her sister Faith, replete with details of behavior of her own and her other sister's children—and said with studied indifference, "Indeed." The apparent lack of interest was calculated to goad her aunt.

Lady Trentower was duly miffed. She continued in an aggressive tone of voice, "It was not enough that she bring scandal to my family. Now she wants to make herself respectable. Well, I won't help her."

Chastity pricked her ears, but refused to give her aunt the satisfaction of requesting the identity of the offending creature. "Umm," she said, but remained alert.

Lady Trentower snorted with exasperation. "I should think you would show a little more concern. After all, she is trying to insinuate herself into a family that is yours as well as mine."

Chastity directed a cool gaze at her aunt. "I do not understand," she said languidly, conveying that an effort to understand was beneath her.

"You'll understand soon enough when she's perched on your doorstep," said Lady Trentower.

Still Chastity refused to give her aunt the satisfaction of asking who she was talking about. She smiled slightly, shrugged and went back to reading her own letter, though by this time she was tense with curiosity.

"She is, you know, your other aunt," continued Lady Trentower, a sour look on her face.

"Are you speaking of Evelyn de Brey? I mean, Lady Grasset?" said Chastity, reacting in spite of her effort to remain aloof.

"How many aunts do you have?" said Lady Trentower.

"Is she coming here?" asked Chastity quickly, ignoring her aunt's sarcasm.

"She *wants* to come here. I shall not allow it."

"I hardly think you can keep Lady Grasset out of England," said Chastity, a touch of scorn in her voice.

"Who's talking of England? Let her come to England. I can, however, certainly keep her out of my drawing room. And I intend to do so."

"You mean she wishes to see you?"

"That is precisely what I mean. That is what I have been saying. Have you not been listening? She wishes me to receive her. Here. The woman is daft."

Chastity felt a little thrill. "When is she arriving?"

A deep, injured sigh was the precurser of Lady Trentower's answer. "Child, you do not listen. She is *not* arriving. I shall not receive her."

"I mean when does she arrive in England," said Chastity impatiently.

"Oh, as to that," said Lady Trentower grimly, while glancing at the note she held at a distance as though it smelled bad, "sometime next week. She goes so far as to state the day and hour that she will be able to visit." Lady Trentower looked around her drawing room with amazed outrage. "Imagine! *She* will be able to visit me! The woman is most presumptuous."

"I hardly think," said Chastity, "that you can refuse to see her. She is your sister-in-law, and whatever her past might have been, she was the wife of your brother for more than ten years."

"Ten years. You speak as though that had some significance. What is ten years to me? She was a guttersnipe when my brother married her, and she has remained a guttersnipe as far as I'm concerned. William made a mistake when he legitimatized their quite reprehensible relationship. I shall not add to his folly by pretending to sanction that most unhappy development." Lady Trentower's expression took on a pleasurable vengefulness as she smoothed her skirt.

Chastity could not reconcile her memory of the exquisite Evelyn de Brey with the vehement description of Lady Trentower. "I should think that ten years spent with my uncle, who was the most accomplished and polished gentleman I have ever met, would have eradicated all traces of Miss de Brey's past—unfortunate as it may have been."

"Oh, no doubt there is a veneer there. But the core will remain vulgar and unacceptable," said Lady Trentower, comfortably certain of her judgment.

"When I met Miss de Brey she was not vulgar at all. On the contrary, she was very quiet and withdrawn."

Lady Trentower looked sharply at her niece. "You are defending the woman?"

"I do not think she requires any defense. Certainly not from me."

Lady Trentower's eyes narrowed and she pursed her lips. "Are you suggesting that I open my doors to the woman?"

"I hardly think you can do otherwise."

"Hah!" was Lady Trentower's comment.

"It would look very strange if you were to turn your own sister-in-law away," persisted Chastity, though she retained a dispassionate air.

"Have you thought just what Charles Techett's reaction might be to the return of his former mistress?" asked Lady Trentower with a gleam of spiteful pleasure in her eye.

Chastity had not thought that far. Now that the idea was dangled so unpleasantly before her she thrust out her chin. "I hardly see how Mr. Techett enters the decision as to whether you will receive your sister-in-law," she said stiffly.

"Oh, you don't," said Lady Trentower mockingly, aware that she had uncovered a wound and prepared to rub salt in it. "Well, my dear, if I should be so foolish as to receive my late brother's wife, it would be tantamount to giving her an entrée into the company graced by Charles Techett. And by you." Lady Trentower smiled acidly. "On the other hand, if I do not recognize the creature, she will be doomed to the fringes of society. She will pass her time with the most shabby and ill-regarded hostesses in London. Hostesses, I might add, that your relationship to me has saved you from." She appeared quite pleased at the picture she painted of Evelyn's forthcoming debasement in the less fashionable salons of the city.

"I daresay Lady Grasset could survive exposure to mediocre society," said Chastity coolly.

"Yes. Most likely she wouldn't know the difference. But can you and Charles Techett survive exposure to *her?*" Lady Trentower was visibly pleased at this twist the conversation was taking.

In order to show that the question was beneath notice, Chastity countered with one of her own. "Is Lady Grasset coming to England to visit or to live?"

Lady Trentower's expression remained pleased— her eyes were unusually sparkling—as she replied, "She is arriving in the party of the Grand Duchess Catherine, or the Duchess of Oldenburg, as she is sometimes called. She does not state whether she will remain or not."

Chastity could not suppress her surprise. All the papers had been filled with the impending visit of the Grand Duchess Catherine, who was the beloved, the favorite, sister of Tsar Alexander the First of Russia. Her visit was apparently a harbinger of the arrival of the Tsar himself, and she had engaged all of the Pulteney Hotel, at the incredible sum of 250 guineas a week, for herself and her retinue. If Lady Grasset was part of this no doubt magnificent and important visit, she must be very well thought of in Russia. Chastity briefly wondered whether someone so highly regarded really needed her championship. Her aunt's barb about Charles Techett added to her doubt. But she had committed herself to a course, and she was not one to waver in the face of untoward disclosures; she refused to allow mere facts to influence her feelings. "In that case," she said with asperity, "it seems to me that an insult to Lady Grasset would be particularly unwise, for it would reflect upon her patroness, the Grand Duchess."

Lady Trentower shrugged. "I have no interest whatsoever in the Grand Duchess's sensibilities. Any woman who would add a streetsinger to her retinue cannot be very discriminating."

Chastity's tongue clicked with annoyance. "Lady Grasset, I must repeat, has had the benefit of ten years' exposure to your brother. She is, furthermore, a great beauty. Whatever else she is, she is not just a former streetsinger at this juncture of her life. That she has been taken up by the sister of the Tsar of Russia surely testifies to the fact."

"Oh, Russians," said Lady Trentower disdainfully. "What do they know about breeding?"

"Must I remind you, aunt, that it was Russians who were our greatest ally in defeating Napoleon?" Chastity spoke these words ponderously, in a rather dishonest appeal to a patriotism that she herself did not feel very strongly, but to which she knew Lady Trentower was susceptible.

There was a slight waver in the old woman's voice to signal that Chastity had scored a point. "I daresay we would have eventually fixed that little man on our own," she said, but without her usual forcefulness.

"The fact remains that we did not, however, and that the Russians are our allies. Valued allies. Furthermore, if Lady Grasset is arriving in London under such illustrious patronage, it does not seem to me likely that your forbidding her access to your drawing room is going to have a very great impact upon her reception by society."

Lady Trentower bristled. "My influence in London society is considerably greater than any Russian Grand Duchess's." But she was not as assured as she had been. Uncertainty made her querulous.

Chastity, sensing a crumbling of defenses, bore home. "No doubt," she said dryly, with just the proper touch of skepticism, carefully avoiding a show of outright disbelief. "However, might it not be more gracious to receive Lady Grasset as representative of a valued ally if not as a sister-in-law? Surely such a gesture would be appreciated not only by Lady Grasset, but also by the Grand Duchess, and even the Prince Regent."

Lady Trentower guarded her disturbed frown, and fidgeted with her skirt. "We shall see," she said shortly.

Chastity knew then that she had won the point.

Chapter Two

Lady Trentower was not insensitive, nor was she obtuse. She did have, however, a marked mischievous streak, and this occasionally led her into behavior that smacked of both conditions. When Charles Techett called later, on the day she received the letter from Lady Grasset, it was this sense of mischief that prompted her to direct the conversation down paths that most thoughtful people would have avoided.

"So, my dear Charles, I wonder if you can guess who I have had news of today?"

Charles Techett looked at her calmly; he was composed and faintly amused. He put his cup on the saucer with a quiet clink and smiled. Chastity, watching with some apprehension to gauge his reaction, admired at the same time the way his black hair curled over his high white forehead, and the seemingly artless fashion in which his impeccable stock framed his face.

"Do you really wish me to guess, Lady Trentower?" he asked in a deep teasing voice. "Or shall I simply capitulate and confess I haven't the slightest idea?"

"I doubt if you could guess," said Lady Trentower, gleeful malice shining in her eyes. "So I shall not put you to the test. Lady Grasset. I had a letter from Lady Grasset today."

Not a flicker of surprise touched Charles Techett's face, nor did his smile waver. He inclined his head slightly and said, "How interesting. So did I."

"You?" said Lady Trentower, her good humor instantly doused. "The impertinence of the woman. Whatever did she want?"

Chastity was acutely uncomfortable. "Surely," she said, attempting lightness, "that is no business of ours."

"Of course it is our business," said Lady Trentower sharply. "It is a family matter."

"Are you worried about your sister-in-law?" asked Charles Techett with seriocomic concern.

"I am worried about the good name of my brother, and what that woman does can reflect upon it," answered Lady Trentower sternly. Her rectitude was not sufficiently convincing to disguise her pique at having failed to nonplus Charles Techett.

"I assure you," said Charles, guarding his air of calm amusement, "that Lady Grasset's letter in no way demeaned her late husband nor herself."

"But what did she *want?*" persisted Lady Trentower aggressively.

"She sent her greetings and announced that she would be arriving in London next week. That is all," said Charles with a graceful gesture that diminished the importance of his statement.

"That is all!" said Lady Trentower. "That seems extremely forward to me." She straightened and primly crimped her lips. "Under the circumstances," she added significantly.

Her innuendo did not appear to touch Charles. He continued smiling pleasantly as he answered,

"Not at all. We are, you may remember, old friends, and it is always pleasant to hear from old friends. You," he nodded to Lady Trentower, "never met Evelyn—or Lady Grasset I suppose I must call her now—but I think you'll find her agreeable enough."

"That would astonish me mightily," said Lady Trentower.

"I believe you have met Lady Grasset," said Charles to Chastity. "What was your opinion?" He asked the question as casually as if they were all gossiping about an individual they had encountered in the pages of a gazette, rather than someone who had touched, with varying degrees of intimacy, all their lives.

It was not a question that Chastity could answer honestly in that company. How could she reply that Evelyn de Brey had become for her the symbol of true and tragic love and the most interesting woman she had ever met? Furthermore, had she been compelled to speak the truth, she would have had to add that it was because of Charles Techett's distressing need to cast her off that had, in a sense, conferred this prominence on her. So she said simply, "She was—or is, I suppose, still—very beautiful, and very quiet."

Her aunt looked at her sourly, as if to say her statement was namby-pamby. Charles continued smiling, and nodded impersonally, neither agreeing nor disagreeing. The pause stretched uncomfortably long.

Finally Lady Trentower exhaled sharply and said, "Well, the woman has insinuated herself into the good graces of the Tsar's sister—for what that's worth. Not much, I suspect. The Grand

Duchess is reputed to be 'clever.'" She said the last word in a pinched, disapproving manner.

Charles continued smiling. "In the ten years or so since Lady Grasset has been abroad I imagine she has become clever also. Or at least considerably more so than when she left England."

Lady Trentower disliked this judgment every bit as much as that of Chastity, and favored Charles with the same sour look. Then she rose abruptly and said, "I have much to do this afternoon, so I shall not linger over tea. I leave you both alone." She paused an instant, looking sharply at Chastity, before adding, "It's not as if you needed a chaperone. You are, after all, both quite mature."

Though Chastity was accustomed to her aunt's sharp tongue, this parting shot drew blood. She blushed from embarrassment, and then blushed even more as she realized she was blushing.

Charles appeared to notice nothing unusual. He maintained his calm amusement as he stood to watch Lady Trentower leave the room, and then settled back into the chair facing Chastity.

"Would you care for more tea?" she asked after a brief strained silence.

"Thank you," he said affably, and smiled, looking directly into her eyes.

As she poured and offered the cup, he said, "You have chosen an interesting time to visit London, what with the arrival of Russian royalty and the like."

"Yes. I am sure the visitors will be most interesting." She was embarrassed at the inanity of her remark; to cover her confusion she began to putter, dumping the dregs into the slop basin, and spooning fresh tea into the pot.

"It will be amusing to hear Lady Grasset's views on the Grand Duchess," said Charles pleasantly.

Chastity glanced quickly at him. She could not reconcile his casual attitude toward Lady Grasset with her image of him as Evelyn de Brey's desperate lover of a decade ago. She wondered whether he was dissimulating. If so, he was doing an excellent job of it.

"Yes, I daresay she will have much of interest to tell us... about Russia and her life there." Chastity did not seem to be able to avoid stilted phrases. She was annoyed at her constraint, and began to bang the tea things about with more ferocity than was necessary.

"Oh," said Charles airily, "I wouldn't expect any very enlightening observations from her if I were you. Though I teased your aunt with the prospect of a clever Lady Grasset appearing on the scene, I would be most surprised if that proved to be the case."

"Why is that?" asked Chastity, all animation suddenly suspended.

"Evelyn, when she left England at least, was not particularly bright." Charles made this statement in an offhanded way, as though it were a well-known truism.

Chastity was dismayed. Charles and Evelyn had been enshrined in her private pantheon for so long that now to hear the former pass such unflattering judgment on the latter was tantamount to hearing Abelard declare that Héloïse really was not very interesting.

"I had a different impression of her," she said

hesitantly, all the while remembering that Evelyn's intelligence or lack of it had never been a source of speculation before.

"I daresay," said Charles, "since she only spent two or three days with your family. Had she stayed longer you would have come to a different conclusion." He looked up at the ceiling a moment before adding, "Actually, she was so exquisite that one just assumed all her other faculties must be on a par with her appearance. It was too painful to contemplate the possibility that she might be flawed in some area."

"I see," said Chastity. She was torn between wanting to hear more and distaste at Charles's ungallant attitude. The thought that perhaps Charles had not been as much in love with Evelyn as she had supposed—as, indeed, all London had supposed—arose; she looked more carefully at him. "I was under the impression," she said hesitantly, "that you and she were very closely linked." As soon as she had spoken she regretted the statement. As it echoed through her head it sounded so prying.

Charles showed no sign he found her remark out of line. On the contrary, he laughed with a sort of intimate ease and his manner remained light and almost frivolous as he replied, "Indeed we were. Ours was the sort of love that, I suspect, only people in their early twenties can experience—and then only if they are fortunate enough to find someone who will share it with them. It is also the sort of love one inevitably outgrows."

Chastity paused before asking tentatively, "You no longer feel the same toward Evelyn, then?"

Charles laughed with genuine amusement.

"Good heavens, no! It would be an astounding feat of emotional force to sustain such a feeling for more than a few months, at most. Evelyn and I were separated by circumstances before our ardor naturally dissipated. Consequently we pined longer than we would have otherwise. But certainly I did not carry my sighs very far into my marriage." A physician dissecting a corpse could not have spoken more disinterestedly. He looked at Chastity with amusement. "Surely, Miss Dalrymple, you no longer shelter the same intense flame that once blazed for *your* first love?"

Chastity was faced with the unpleasant choice of admitting she had never actually kindled the blaze Charles alluded to so lightly, or of pretending through her silence that her past was a series of veritable conflagrations. Honesty dictated the former course, and she said rather primly, "I cannot speak from experience, sir. I have never been involved in such entanglements." She was blushing again, from vexation at having to confess her lack of firsthand knowledge in the sacred realm of the emotions. That most of society did not regard her lack as a shortcoming, but quite the contrary, did not matter. The thought that this conversation was not going well crossed her mind.

Charles, however, seemed at ease, and even interested. "I am delighted to meet one of those fortunate people whose heads always hold their hearts in firm control. You are obviously too sensible to have allowed yourself to fall into that abyss of desperate love where one can plunge with such devastating results."

He could not have wounded Chastity more painfully. She had passed most of her life believing that her emotions were wild, untamed and potent. She had felt superior to Faith and Hope because they had settled for colorless and plodding spouses while she, unbridled spirit that she was, waited for the gallant who had dash, romance, color, spirit. Now, suddenly, Charles Techett had presented a sketch that revealed her as calculating and restrained as her sisters. On the surface, she had to admit, the facts bore him out. The impartial observer of her uncluttered life could hardly come to any conclusion other than that she had kept her heart under strictest discipline. What was not apparent was that she had been hindered by a lack of acceptable suitors. She could not point this out, however, without sounding defensive or apologetic. There was, in fact, no suitable rejoinder, so she smiled enigmatically.

"Perhaps," said Charles, suddenly grown serious, "I have trespassed into an area where I have no business. Forgive me if I have been forward."

"Not at all," said Chastity simply. "I have no objections to your remarks. It's just that... I have not the proper answers to them."

Charles laughed. "Proper? What would the proper answers be?"

She raised her eyebrows quizzically. "I have spent my time away from London and am not versed in city badinage. I don't know what the answers to such gallant remarks should be. If I did I would give them."

A look that was distinctly tender came over Charles and he leaned forward as he said, "I assure you, Miss Dalrymple, that I find your discourse, as everything else about you, not only quite proper but absolutely charming."

Chastity lowered her eyes briefly before replying, "Thank you, sir. I value your good opinion." The moment assumed great significance as the silence remained unbroken. Then Charles, like one shaking himself back to the everyday world, said, "I fear I have overstayed my time. I will be off before I begin to bore you."

"That would not be possible," said Chastity, giving him her hand and a smile.

"Even so, I don't wish to risk not being welcome the next time I come," he said, standing over her and looking down into her eyes.

"You know you will always be welcome, Mr. Techett," said Chastity with what was, she felt, the right mixture of reserve and encouragement. He bowed and left.

Chastity, thinking back, found some fault with her visitor—he was not very discreet about his former mistress, and certainly was not gallant in her regard—yet on the whole she was inclined to be favorably disposed toward him. In fact, she felt a little tremor of nerves, a slight rush of pleasure; she could not remember ever having experienced these symptoms before. She spent a great part of the afternoon savoring the details of their conversation, and devising more polished repartee for future exchanges.

Her reverie was interrupted by Lady Trentower, who had grown bored with her own affairs and sought out her niece. "Alone, I see," she said, as though it were an accusation. "When did Charles leave?"

"Some time ago," said Chastity.

"Did he have anything interesting to say?" asked Lady Trentower significantly.

Chastity knew very well what she meant, but chose to take the question at face value. "No. We talked only of general matters."

"There was no subtle understanding that passed between you?"

"No."

"Ah. Well, then I suppose you've lost your advantage there. It's to be expected, what with that woman showing up after all these years. I imagine he'll go hightailing it back to her, now that they're both rich and free."

The pleasant glow surrounding Charles's image disappeared as Chastity felt a little stab of anxiety. "I question that," she said tartly. "He no longer harbors any affection for Evelyn."

"He said that?" asked Lady Trentower, her interest quickened.

Chastity regretted having exposed herself to her aunt's inquisitiveness, but since it was done she had no recourse but to continue. "Not in so many words. He merely said that his liaison with Evelyn de Brey had taken place when they were both much younger."

"I hardly call that revelatory," said Lady Trentower disdainfully. "All London knows that."

"What he meant," explained Chastity with annoyance, "was that their affair was such that only young people can indulge in. Now they are both beyond the age of infatuation."

"Hah!" said Lady Trentower. "He's a fool if he really believes that. I've seen infatuation in men of eighty. Beyond the age of infatuation indeed. What nonsense."

"He said that the feeling between himself and

Lady Grasset had disappeared," insisted Chastity with some asperity.

"That's because she disappeared. Now she will reappear, and you can be sure that their feeling will too. At the very least they will want to put each other to the test. Mark my words," said Lady Trentower gaily.

Chastity was stung with doubt. Suddenly, in the light of her aunt's analysis, it seemed highly improbable that the participants in one of the great love affairs of the past decade would be satisfied just to shake hands and reminisce a bit upon finding each other again. She could not keep her distress from showing, and Lady Trentower looked at her shrewdly.

"Are you sure, my dear, that Charles gave you no encouragement?" she asked, her curiosity thinly glazed with concern. "You seem to be uncommonly interested in his attitude toward his former mistress."

"You forget that I met Lady Grasset when she was Evelyn de Brey. Of course I am interested."

"Hmm. Mere inquisitiveness seems to make you very fidgety."

"I assure you I am nothing of the sort," said Chastity with sufficient force to confirm her aunt's judgment.

"Delighted to be proven wrong, my dear," said Lady Trentower drily. Then, brightening her voice several shades, "Well, we have something now to look forward to. In a sense we shall be participating in the arrival of the Russians, what with a distant, *very* distant, relative in the entourage. I shall start paying more attention to those tiresome accounts in the journals."

She chattered on for several moments; Chastity paid her no mind, but sat pensively looking at the tea table.

During the next few days all the journals, newspapers and gazettes were crammed with news of the arrival of the Duchess of Oldenburg. Almost all that was printed was speculation—as to what she would wear, who she would visit, where she would entertain and so on—but the few solid facts were impressive. She had, it was confirmed, rented the whole Pulteney Hotel at 250 guineas a week, an extraordinary amount to spend, particularly when one considered that she could have stayed in lodgings provided by the Prince Regent (who was reported piqued that his invitation had been rebuffed). She was, it was almost certain, coming to blaze the trail for the arrival later in the year of her brother the Tsar, and no Tsar or Grand Duke had come to England since Peter the Great in 1698. Since she was recently widowed, and since there was a wealth of talentless royal bachelors among the Prince Regent's brothers and cousins, most papers assumed that she was coming in search of a husband. It was noted in most journals that the Russian ambassador, Count Leiven, was extremely taciturn about her, and from this it was deduced that there was no love lost between them. And rarely did a day go by without one or usually more of the pieces spewed out by the press mentioning that accompanying the Grand Duchess was a widowed English noblewoman, Lady Grasset.

"An English noblewoman," snorted Lady Trentower when meeting with the reference. "Surely they are writing with tongue in cheek."

After such a hullabaloo the Grand Duchess Catherine's entry into London was surprisingly demure. There was no long line of glittering coaches emblazoned with the imperial crest, nor were there legions of cossacks flanking the ordinary vehicles that had been rented to transport the duchess and her party to the city. The newspapers were quite disappointed, in fact, and one stated that the Grand Duchess herself hardly measured up to her English counterparts. (The journalist was, one assumed, speaking of the Prince Regent's rather lackluster sisters.) She arrived on the thirty-first of March. On the first of April Lady Trentower received a brief note confirming the fact that Lady Grasset would wait upon her at Lady Trentower's residence on the following day.

"She is impertinent," said Lady Trentower. "It might not suit me at all to see her. She should have thought of that." She was not entirely reconciled to receiving her sister-in-law, and was still toying with the idea of closing her drawing room to her. Finally, however, she did not, for curiosity won over rectitude. So on the morning of the second of April both Lady Trentower and Chastity were taut with anticipation, though each was careful to disguise the fact from the other.

By early afternoon, when Lady Grasset was due, they had wandered to the drawing room. The windows faced the street, but neither woman would permit herself to peek through the curtains as long as the other was present, so they sat, stiffening each time a coach went clattering by below.

The hour for Lady Grasset's arrival approached and departed with no sign of her. Lady Trentower shifted in her chair, and grew more glum as the minutes crept by; a quarter hour after her guest was due she rose abruptly to her feet.

"I shall instruct Thomas to say I am not at home," she said. Thomas was her butler, and at that moment he opened the door to the drawing room to announce gravely:

"Lady Grasset and Count Orlanov have arrived, ma'am."

"Who? Who?" said Lady Trentower, disturbed by the addition of a guest she was not expecting. Thomas did not have time to reply, for two extraordinary creatures came sweeping past him into the room and bore down on the startled old woman with such momentum that she took a step backward in order to avoid collision.

Lady Grasset made a deep theatrical bow in front of Lady Trentower, and rose, saying, "Dear sister, at last we meet."

Chastity stared incredulously at the woman in order to make sure that it was indeed the former Evelyn de Brey. She had grown enormously fat. Though her dress was black, as befitted a widow, it was ornately embellished, and cut low over a vast expanse of creamy white bosom. The hair was as black and glistening as ever, and the eyes as lustrous, but the latter were surrounded by folds of superfluous flesh, and jowels framed the tiny, perfect mouth.

Lady Trentower, who had been expecting to see something quite different, and who was, in addition, rattled at being called "sister," was momentarily routed into speechlessness. She stood, her hand pressed against her bony chest and stared at the billowing woman.

Her silence permitted Lady Grasset to command the situation, and she turned to Chastity with a gracious, magnanimous gesture worthy of a diva. "I am Evelyn, Lady Grasset," she said with a good imitation of humility.

"I am Chastity Dalrymple. We met some years ago at Grangeford, where you passed through on your way to Russia."

"Ah, yes," said Lady Grasset. "Of course." It was apparent she had no recollection of Chastity. Her eyes had that vague polite cast to them that indicated she probably did not even remember Grangeford.

"And this," Lady Grasset continued, turning to her companion, "is Count Peter Orlanov."

The count clicked his heels and bowed sharply from the waist. He was superb: tall and blond, with a luxurious moustache that spiked masterfully upwards on either side of his mouth, and icy blue eyes that bore through whatever they settled on. He was dressed in a white, gold-trimmed uniform that outlined every contour of his torso and thighs, and glistening black boots that delineated his muscular calves. On his left arm he carried a white casque, from the center of which a scarlet plume of feathers spurted as though an artery had been pierced. Standing erectly behind Lady Grasset, he was a white, gold and crimson pillar.

Lady Trentower recovered, but only to the extent of proffering an icy, "How d'you do?" directed at both her visitors.

"Won't you have tea?" asked Chastity, taking over for her aunt who seemed indisposed to assume the duties of hostess.

"How charming," said Lady Grasset. "An English tea! You are in for a treat, Peter," she added looking at her tall, golden escort. Then turning back to Lady Trentower, as though it had been she who had issued the invitation, continued, "How thoughtful of you. One of the things dear William and I missed most at Saint Petersburg was the English tea. Oh," she waved her hand dismissively, "we introduced the custom at court, and the dear Tsar and Tsarina frequently joined us in our little collations—but it was not the same thing as a real English tea. Caviar and sturgeon are all very well in their place, but one can have surfeit of them. So now we are to be regaled with the genuine thing." She beamed at Lady Trentower, who continued to glower.

Lady Grasset settled on one of the small chairs placed near the tea table, and so completely obscured it that she appeared to be nestling among her own bulk. Count Orlanov quickly and decisively took a seat to her right and a little behind her; his inflexible back remained at least two inches from the gilded back of the chair.

Chastity poured and passed the cups while Lady Grasset continued to chatter animatedly, directing almost all her comments to a persistently dour Lady Trentower. When she fell silent to sip her tea, or, possibly, just to catch her breath, it was Chastity who took over the task of fueling the conversation, since her aunt seemed incapable, or unwilling, to do so.

"And how long do you think you will stay?" she asked during one of these pauses.

"If I have my way I shall stay forever. But I may not be able to—for in spite of one's wishing it weren't so, one still has obligations." She sounded regretful, as though a duty hung heavily over her head. To make certain that her sister-in-law siezed the point she gave a long deep sigh. Lady Trentower responded with a glacial stare at nothing at all.

"Well, then," said Chastity, "you will be staying at the Pulteney with the Grand Duchess for the next few weeks, I suppose."

"For the next few *months*. We are here, in a manner of speaking, to prepare the way for the visit of the Tsar," said Lady Grasset impressively.

"How very fascinating," said Chastity, "to be part of such a mission."

"I cannot deny there is much satisfaction in such a role," said Lady Grasset demurely, "but at the same time there is much responsibility."

Lady Trentower stirred and asked skeptically, "Just what are *you* responsible for?"

Lady Grasset was so gratified at being addressed by her sister-in-law that she overlooked the tone of the question. "The Grand Duchess is unaccustomed to our English ways, in spite of the fact that she is a most cultured, intelligent and educated woman. In a sense I am her guide through the intricate customs and society of my dear native land."

Lady Trentower gave her an appalled stare. Before she could supplement her reaction with a comment, Chastity hastened to say, "That is indeed a delicate position for you to be in."

"It is the least I can do for two countries that have been so good to me," said Lady Grasset modestly.

"How exactly are you guiding your Grand Duchess?" asked Lady Trentower distastefully.

"Ah. That is one of the reasons—only one, I assure you—why I wished to see you today. Of course, I was eager to embrace my dear sister for her own sake, but at the same time I also wanted to invite you personally to a ball the Grand Duchess is giving next week. You will receive an invitation from her, of course, but I am acting as a kind of herald, carrying the news from one eminent lady to another, the way bees visit the blossoms. You, my dear sister, are one of the most eminent of ladies in society, and so we—the Grand Duchess and myself—are most eager to see you there." Lady Grasset smiled brilliantly. Her teeth, Chastity noted, were still white and even.

Lady Trentower looked as if she would burst with indignation. Chastity said, "I should think a ball at this time of the year would be most welcome, since there has been little such activity lately."

"Oh, we know this is not the season, but we do not wish to wait to introduce the Grand Duchess to the widest range of notable citizens. You, of course," she turned sweetly to Lady Trentower, "fall well within that range."

"Indeed," said Lady Trentower in a strangled voice.

"Now I suppose we must part," said Lady Grasset with lively good humor. "We don't want to wear out our welcome, and furthermore we must carry the tidings to others." She rose, and Chastity was amazed at the grace with which she managed so much excess flesh. "I look forward to seeing you again soon, dear sister. And you, also," she added turning to Chastity with a bright smile. "The Grand Duchess has not yet set aside an afternoon for receiving, but as soon as she does you will be apprised of the fact. And, of course, we shall meet at the ball next week." Then, quick as a bird, she leaned forward over Lady Trentower and gave her a kiss on the cheek. "*Au revoir*," she said gaily and sailed out of the room. Her size gave her departure a certain majesty. Count Orlanov bowed twice from the waist, clicked his heels and strode after her, the scarlet feathers of his casque bobbing as he went. He had not said a single word.

Chapter Three

Lady Trentower sat stunned for several moments. Then she inhaled deeply. "Well!"

"She is much changed," said Chastity cautiously. "She has become stout."

"Stout? She is not stout. She is not plump. She is fat. Fat. Fat. Fat," said Lady Trentower vehemently. "And she comes barging into my drawing room calling me sister, and dragging that savage after her."

"Count Orlanov?" said Chastity surprised. "He is a very handsome man."

"He is notably lacking in conversation," said Lady Trentower, as though she had been insulted by the count's silence.

"Perhaps he doesn't speak English."

"Then let him stay at home, or remain in that hotel they have appropriated."

"It seemed to me that he had little opportunity to speak. No one, I believe, addressed him except Lady Grasset in passing."

"*She*, I suppose you might say, spoke quite enough for both of them. How the woman babbled! A bee visiting blossoms indeed. Did you ever hear such foolishness?"

"The image was unfortunate, but not malicious, at least."

"Her Grand Duchess," continued Lady Trentower grimly, "is in a pretty pickle indeed if that is to be her emissary to London society."

"I daresay that most people will not be so distressed as you. Your connection with her had prejudiced you against her. Others will be quite happy to receive news of a ball given by the Grand Duchess."

Lady Trentower spoke with animosity. "I do hope you are not going to persist in defending that woman after the display she has made here this afternoon."

With a little tremor of surprise, Chastity realized that she was indeed championing Lady Grasset. She quickly recognized that it was relief that brought her to this position. She had been disturbed when she heard that Lady Grasset was returning and her aunt had declared that Charles would no doubt rush back to her side. Now that she had seen what had become of the exquisite Evelyn she was no longer distressed. She was eager for Charles to see her as soon as possible.

Though she perceived her motive, and silently admitted her aunt was correct, she replied, "I can see no reason to defend Lady Grasset. She seems quite capable of taking care of herself."

"If audacity is any guarantee of success, certainly she shall take the town by storm," said Lady Trentower.

"Well, she is bringing very good connections with her."

"You mean the Russians?" asked Lady Trentower scornfully.

"I think most people will be eager to meet the Grand Duchess."

"*I* am not. Nor am I curious. If the sister of the

Tsar has to rely upon a streetsinger to guide her through society she cannot be very worthy."

"Surely you will not refuse the Grand Duchess's invitations?"

"I most certainly shall. I won't be used—that is what the creature is trying to do, use her family ties to me to insinuate herself and that Russian into decent drawing rooms. I will not allow it." Lady Trentower stiffened in her seat and glared at her niece, waiting for defiance. Chastity chose to remain calm, reasonable and sweet-tempered. She surmised, rightly, that this would be the line of behavior best calculated to annoy her aunt. She began to tidy the tea things with an expression of gentle forbearance.

"It's all very well for you to indulge your curiosity," said Lady Trentower aggressively, "for you are here today and gone tomorrow. I, however, have obligations to society. I cannot give my approval to every adventuress who takes it into her head to install herself in our midst. I have to maintain standards. You can blithely walk away, but I have to live with the consequences of my behavior."

"I would hardly call the sister of the Tsar an adventuress, nor, for that matter, is Lady Grasset. She was married for ten years to your brother and that, it seems to me, should be quite sufficient credentials for her entry into society." Chastity continued to toy gently with the tea service.

"William was not, alas, infallible," said Lady Trentower with finality. "What's more, you can rest assured that society will not be taken in by either the Grand Duchess or her *friend*. I doubt that Lady Grasset will be received in any decent house in London."

Lady Trentower was wrong, as she learned the following day when Charles Techett paid a call. He arrived, urbane and affable, and impeccably groomed. He had hardly taken a seat before Lady Trentower spoke.

"Well, Charles, I suppose you have heard about Lady Grasset?" She studied him, a malicious glint in her eye.

"I have more than heard about her. I have met with her and had a very pleasant chat."

"No!" said Lady Trentower, shocked. "You mean she came to call on you?"

"No," said Charles smoothly, with a slight smile. "I met her while taking tea with Lady Bradford."

This news upset Lady Trentower even more. "Lady Bradford has received her?" she asked sharply.

"Why, yes, as have Lady Buford and Lady Holland—so far. No doubt there are many more who will be seeing her shortly."

The names were impressive, and Lady Trentower was distressed. "What can they be thinking of?" she said almost to herself.

"Right now," said Charles, "they are thinking of the ball to be given by the Grand Duchess next week."

"They're going?" asked Lady Trentower incredulously.

"Certainly. They would be very unhappy if they were not. The Grand Duchess's invitation is one of the most vied for in London." Charles spoke innocently, as though he were unaware of the turmoil he was raising in Lady Trentower's breast.

"And you? Are you going?" persisted Lady Trentower, sounding like an inquisitor.

"I assure you I shall see you there," said Charles with aplomb.

Lady Trentower was too taken aback to protest, and she lapsed into silence to mull over this development.

Chastity was longing to ask Charles his impression of Lady Grasset, but could not without being, she feared, indelicate. She was wondering how she could change the subject when Charles broke the silence his news had precipitated. "It appears that Russia agreed with Lady Grasset," he said blandly.

"Yes," replied Chastity, somewhat at a loss. "She seems quite blooming."

"At least," said Lady Trentower, finding her tongue, "the climate did not interfere with her appetite."

"No," said Charles pleasantly, as though the remark had been an innocent observation. "It is apparent that she adapted quite well."

"She must have spent her time gobbling up everything in sight," said Lady Trentower ungraciously.

Charles smiled agreeably, but said nothing.

Though Chastity was embarrassed at her aunt's rancor, she was interested in Charles's reaction to it. She could not fathom what he felt—whether he had been dismayed by the changes in the formerly sylph-like Evelyn, or whether he was indifferent to them. His facade was so carefully constructed that it was impossible to peek beyond it.

After allowing the pause to stretch a few seconds longer, he said to Chastity, "I hope that you, also, will attend the ball."

"I have no idea whether I shall be invited," said Chastity quietly. "Lady Grasset addressed herself mainly to my aunt."

"I'm sure," said Charles, "you are on the Grand Duchess's list. It is her desire to meet everyone who is noteworthy in London, and certainly you qualify."

"How kind...," began Chastity softly, when Lady Trentower interrupted, "Was that savage with her at Lady Bradford's?"

"Do you mean Count Orlanov?" said Charles, and Chastity noticed a slight distaste cross his features. "Yes. He accompanied Lady Grasset."

"Just what is that relationship?" asked Lady Trentower belligerently. "Who is the man and what is he to her?"

"I am not aware of any particular relationship between them," said Charles stiffly. "I suppose he is merely acting as Lady Grasset's escort while she pays her visits."

"Hmm," said Lady Trentower dubiously.

Charles Techett's dislike of Count Orlanov was obvious to Chastity, and she wondered whether it stemmed from jealousy; it was just possible that he was not as unmoved by Evelyn's reappearance as he pretended. But then surely, she thought, searching for reassurance, surely Charles would be repelled by the transformation of his former mistress. She had returned to him weighing at least fifty, or maybe seventy-five, pounds more than when she had left. The cloud of ill-humor passed from his features as she watched; again there was no indication of his feelings.

He returned to Chastity. "Though it is early to ask, and you may accuse me of being importunate, I hope you will honor me with a dance or two?"

"With greatest pleasure. Although I fear that I am not a very accomplished dancer," said Chastity. In fact, in the vicinity of Grangeford she was considered a most lively and graceful partner, and it was often remarked that Miss Dalrymple moved like a nymph. She was aware of this opinion, and secretly shared it. But that was at Grangeford, and she did not know what would be expected in a London ballroom, so she chose to denigrate her abilities in order that they would show in a better light when the time came to reveal them.

"I cannot imagine," said Charles gallantly, "that you would be anything but elegant on the ballroom floor, the same as you are everywhere else."

Chastity smiled shyly, and quickly glanced directly into his eyes.

"It's just possible," said Lady Trentower as though no one had spoken, "that I shall go to the ball in order to inspect the Grand Duchess for myself." She looked at Chastity and Charles defiantly.

"That is most gracious of you," said Charles politely.

"The woman *is* a visitor to these shores," continued Lady Trentower, "and she comes from what I understand to be a very backward country. How was she to know that she was insulting me by sending that companion of hers to pave the way?"

"Surely you don't mean Lady Grasset," said Charles equably.

"Yes. That is exactly who I mean," said Lady Trentower.

Chastity said, "I found Lady Grasset's visit most interesting, and am looking forward to seeing her again." She smiled serenely as her aunt glared. Charles remained pleasant and after a few protestations that he was anticipating with delight meeting them both next week, he departed.

The following day the invitations arrived, one addressed to Lady Trentower, and a separate one to Chastity. Both were promptly accepted, and the two women began their preparations. Chastity ordered a new dress from the seamstress her aunt had recommended when she first arrived. Lady Trentower at first asserted that she would wear whatever happened to fall under hand on the evening of the ball; but then the papers began to print so much speculation about the event, and her friends were so unabashedly excited that she, too, commanded a new gown. "I shall be able to use it for the season," she said by way of justification. Charles Techett sent a note inquiring whether he might accompany them, and that invitation was accepted also.

"It is possible that he is still somewhat interested in you," mused Lady Trentower. "In which case we should encourage him."

Chastity found the condescension maddening, but did not reply.

The evening of the ball the two women met in the foyer just before Charles was due and inspected each other critically. Chastity had to admit that for a septuagenarian her aunt was still handsome. Though rather gaunt, she had artfully draped her frame in gray silk, and was cautious about exposing her bosom and arms. She wore the most splendid rubies—a necklace, long earrings and a diadem—that Chastity had ever seen, and it was mostly because of these that her compliments were sincere.

Chastity could afford to be generous, for she knew that she looked extremely fetching herself. Her gown was of several layers of diaphanous white muslin that was gathered under her breasts and fell in a straight line to her ankles. The neckline was scooped quite low, and showed her bosom to advantage. The only trim was the most delicate band of white lace around the neck and hem. She wore a modest diamond necklace and two small matching earrings. Her hair, brushed to a gloss, curled in a seemingly careless fashion over her forehead and around her ears. Her color was heightened subtly by lip rouge and the faintest blush of cochineal on her cheeks. Excitement made her eyes sparkle.

"You look *très jeune fille*," said Lady Trentower grudgingly.

Chastity found the praise somewhat double-edged, but she acknowledged it with a slight smile and cool nod. Charles Techett arrived garbed in black coat and trousers and dazzling white cravat, and exclaimed over the beauty of both of them. He looked at Chastity with open and unabashed admiration. Then they set off for the Pulteney Hotel.

During the ride Lady Trentower grumbled, much as though she were being forced to attend against her will. "Well," she said philosophically as they approached Picadilly, "I suppose that now

I've come this far I might as well go through with it." Her companions murmured agreement.

Their coach fell into a long line winding toward the entrance of the Pulteney Hotel, which was blazing with light from every window. It was an unusually warm evening for April, and from the open windows of the second floor music trilled to the street. Up the stairs men and women gorgeously cloaked and beplumed moved in a stream of multi-colored splendor, accented by the flash of jewels and the occasional daub of a red uniform. Soon Charles's carriage reached the entry, and its three occupants joined the flow.

They snaked their way through a plain foyer and up an unprepossessing staircase. To the right was the ballroom, and Chastity caught a glimpse of prancing couples lightheartedly stepping through a quadrille. The line, however, was directed toward the left, and wended through a series of antechambers, each leading further from the ballroom and becoming progressively quieter. Finally, by the time they reached the very last chamber, there was not a hint of music to be heard, and the chattering voices had fallen to a hush punctuated by occasional whispers. They stepped into the room, which was brilliantly lighted, and comfortably appointed. At the far end, sitting on a chair that looked rather like a throne, a small woman in black was receiving the passing guests. At first glance she seemed homely, but then her manner and above all her intelligent, lively eyes, redeemed her, and the closer Chastity moved the more imposing she became. To her right, also dressed in black, and wielding an enormous black feather fan, stood Lady Grasset. The mournfulness of her dress was relieved by a dazzling array of diamonds—around her neck, hanging from her ears, clipped into her hair. She glittered like a chandelier.

Standing stiffly behind her in a dark blue uniform with gold braid piqué stood Count Orlanov, his icy blue eyes fixed on the crowd. He was as handsome as Chastity remembered.

Lady Grasset signaled to them as soon as they drew close and said to the Grand Duchess, "Here is my dear sister, about whom you have heard so much." She advanced and gave Lady Trentower a little peck on the cheek, which was not returned. "Her Highness, the Grand Duchess Catherine," said Lady Grasset gracefully.

Grand Duchess Catherine looked sharply at Lady Trentower and then fixed her lively, inquisitive eyes on Chastity and Charles as Lady Grasset repeated their names. She lingered with interest on Charles, as though she were confirming a suspicion, or checking a fact.

"You give me great pleasure," she said to Lady Trentower in perfect English. "I am delighted to meet the sister of my dear friend," she nodded toward Lady Grasset. There was, Chastity was certain, a strain of malicious amusement in her eyes.

Lady Trentower drew herself up to her full height and said, "We are not quite sisters, ma'am," but the protest was muted by the equanimity of the Grand Duchess, who dismissed the remark with a wave of her hand.

"Your brother was one of my dearest friends. He is missed in Saint Petersburg, as you no doubt miss him here." After a slight, sad pause, the

Grand Duchess added, "During my stay here I wish to visit whatever memorial you have erected in his honor."

"I beg your pardon," said Lady Trentower. "Memorial? There is no memorial."

"Is that true?" said the Grand Duchess disapprovingly. "There is one to him in Saint Petersburg—a bust that his widow donated to the Hall of Arts and Sciences, where I have honored it with a wreath. He died, you know, only two months after my own dear husband expired." She looked at Lady Grasset fondly, and without the slightest vestige of sorrow. "We are two lone widows in this cruel world," she said comfortably. Lady Grasset rather melodramatically lowered first her eyes then her head in acquiescence.

The Grand Duchess terminated the show of mourning by briskly continuing the interview. "And now you will go and dance. I am told that all society in England enjoys balls. I detest them. Music has always given me a headache, and when I have been forced to endure it for more than fifteen or at the most twenty minutes, it has made me vomit. Consequently I avoid it." She flashed a quick appraising glance over Chastity. "You, no doubt, enjoy dancing a great deal," she said, and not waiting for an answer continued, "Chastity. That is a strange name. I hope you deserve it." A ripple of amusement crossed her face.

Chastity was embarrassed. She had never liked her name (conferred upon her by a dying mother who, exhausted by a long labor, and weakened by the rapid births of her first two daughters, Faith and Hope, regarded chastity at that point of her life as a virtue more worthwhile than charity) but no one had ever, in her hearing at least, so explicitly drawn attention to its meaning. Now she could only stammer, "Why, yes, of course..."

"Good. Good," said the Grand Duchess merrily and turned to Charles. "Mr. Techett. A widower, I'm told. Here we all are," she made a large gesture that encompassed Lady Grasset and Charles as well as Lady Trentower, "trying to survive our losses." She smiled benignly. "Let us hope that a gracious heaven blesses our efforts."

Lady Trentower, who was standing straighter and straighter, and whose face assumed the expression of someone who is holding her breath, said, "I have managed very well in my widowhood, and can assure you that I am not currently, in any way, trying to survive my losses."

The Grand Duchess studied her briefly. "You English are so cold," she said with a little shrug. Turning to Lady Grasset she added, "Why don't you lead your sister and her friends to the ballroom, madame. There is no need for you to continue attendance on me. I would not wish to deprive you of this reunion with your family and old friends." She smiled meaningfully and glanced at Charles.

Lady Trentower looked as though she were bursting to speak, but instead allowed herself to be led away by Charles. Chastity was on his other arm. Lady Grasset lifted her hand and Count Orlanov rapidly—almost mechanically—moved to her side and extended his arm as a resting place for it. She did not even look at him as she said to the others, "Let us go to the ballroom." She glanced up at Charles through long thick lashes and added, "You remember, sir, you have promised me a dance."

Though it had been ten years since Evelyn de Brey had been declared one of the most beautiful women in the world, and though she had reappeared with an excess of pounds, she still comported herself with all the coquetry, grace and wiles of a beauty. Her assurance was not without foundation. Her flesh, though too ample, was clear, almost translucent, and glowed against her black satin gown like ivory. Her hair was black and glossy and artfully arranged. Her eyes were large and black and lustrous, and thickly fringed. Her gestures were pretty, like those of a dancer, though it was obvious she was striking poses, what with her upraised arm ending in a languid wrist and artfully fanned fingers. She did not look ridiculous because the overall effect was successful. By the time they had reached the ballroom, Chastity was convinced that fat or not, Lady Grasset was indeed still a beauty, and a formidable one.

She was not alone in her conclusion, for as they progressed, others—men, particularly—threw the short fat woman on Count Orlanov's arm glances that lingered appreciatively. Lady Trentower even began to defer slightly to her, though not, in all likelihood, because of her allure, but rather because Lady Grasset was obviously a personage of some importance in this royal, though barbaric, household. Lady Trentower was as susceptible to influence and power as anyone else. Grudgingly she addressed her sister-in-law, "You have good accommodations here, I hope, madame."

"Oh," said Lady Grasset, making a wide sweep

with her black feather fan, "our quarters are cramped after the palaces in Saint Petersburg, but we are managing."

"You resided, then, in the palace?" asked Lady Trentower, carefully keeping her voice neutral.

"Palaces. The Grand Duchess and her brother have many residences—all of which they use regularly," said Lady Grasset airily.

"Did my brother reside at these palaces?" asked Lady Trentower in the same circumspect voice.

"Only off and on. While dearest William was still alive we had our own little home on the canal. But we were, of course, frequent guests of dearest Grand Duchess Catherine. And the Tsar, also," she added for good measure. "Then when William died," she paused a fraction as she lowered her eyes, "my dear friend asked me to come to her for a long visit. I was there when *her* husband, the Duke of Oldenburg, died." Lady Grasset sighed deeply and prettily as she recounted so many tragedies.

"There has been much sorrow in your life," said Charles. Chastity thought she heard a hint of tenderness in his comment.

Lady Grasset raised her eyes to his briefly, and then fluttered her fan across her enormous white bosom. "Indeed there has been," she said in a low voice that for an instant lost all trace of coquetry. Chastity wondered if Charles and she were thinking back to the week eleven years before when they had been forced to part.

Lady Trentower stated forthrightly, "Well, it seems you have learned to cope with whatever sorrow has come your way." They had reached the ballroom, which obviated the necessity for enlarging upon the remark. Chastity assumed her aunt was referring to Lady Grasset's having managed to keep her appetite, and was embarrassed. But Lady Grasset appeared to take the statement as unmitigated homage, and smiled prettily.

The music was lively and the dancers flushed as they skipped and twirled through a reel. The last strains sounded as Lady Grasset, turning to Charles, said, "I hope you won't be embarrassed to dance with someone wearing black?"

"I shall be delighted to dance with you, regardless of what you wear," said Charles, and stepped forward to take her arm, just as the music started up for another reel. They moved onto the floor.

"In my day," said Lady Trentower, "widows in mourning did not even attend balls, much less dance at them."

"I suppose," said Chastity, "the customs are different in Russia."

Lady Trentower looked displeased, but before she had a chance to speak, Count Orlanov bowed from the waist and said,

"Would you honor me, Miss Dalrymple, by dancing with me?"

Both women were as startled as if a mechanical doll had come to life. They had become so accustomed to his mute presence that they regarded him merely as one of the appurtenances of Lady Grasset, like her fan or reticule. Their astonishment was increased by the count's flawless English accent.

"With greatest pleasure," said Chastity, flustered. He raised his arm in the same brisk gesture he had used for Lady Grasset, and Chastity put her hand on it. Together they moved onto the floor and took their places just as the music started.

After the first few bars Chastity lost whatever doubts she had about her ability to hold her own among London dancers, and stepped out with as much artful abandon as ever she had summoned at Grangeford. To add to her delight, Count Orlanov was a superior partner to any she had ever danced with before. Not only was he tall, lithe and strong (his arm around her waist felt like a band of oak), he was also graceful. Exceedingly attentive, he watched her every move, guiding her through the patterns of the reel with consideration; he was protective, and Chastity gave way to the delicious sensation of being cared for.

Her pleasure was enhanced by the awareness that she and Count Orlanov made an extraordinarily handsome couple, and that they were being watched by several pairs of eyes—envious, admiring, spiteful, impressed. She enjoyed being a cynosure, regardless of the judgments she inspired, and she danced all the more spiritedly.

Count Orlanov proved to be much more impressionable than she would have thought. As he warmed to the dance his blue eyes flashed and his lips parted slightly with excitement. He looked admiringly into her face as he bent over to guide her through a turn, and he gave her waist a little more pressure than was necessary as they twirled and turned and pranced and paraded.

The music ended to delighted applause. Both Chastity and Count Orlanov were rosy and breathless, and she laughed from the sheer joy of having exerted herself so successfully.

"Will you take punch with me?" asked the Count.

"I shall be delighted, sir," she answered, fanning herself rapidly.

"You are a superb dancer, Miss Dalrymple," he said as they moved toward the next room where the refreshments were.

"Only when I have a superb partner, sir," said Chastity, smiling at him. She was so pleased with herself that she felt confident enough to indulge in a little gallantry.

"You are too modest. A woman such as yourself makes *any* man excel at whatever he does under her scrutiny. I am quite sure that I, who have never once been in the ocean, could swim from here to France if you were encouraging me."

"What power you invest in me, sir," said Chastity, laughing. "For your sake I am glad that all I require for the moment is a cup of punch."

Count Orlanov excused himself and worked through the press around the refreshment table. In a few moments he was back at Chastity's side with two cups. "Shall we move over there, ma'am?" he suggested, indicating a little alcove.

Chastity agreed without a second thought, and they strolled to the chairs and sat. The candelabra of the room cast a slight shadow in the niche, but it was by no means obscure, and Chastity felt quite at ease. It was obvious that the count was becoming more and more pleased with her company, as she was with his. When she first saw him he had appeared so formidable in his white and gold uniform with the scarlet cockade, and so improbably handsome that she thought surely he had nothing more to offer the world than his looks.

She had not met many extremely handsome men, but the few she had come across had not held up well under scrutiny: either they were vain or shallow or both. Their appearance was their contribution to society, and they made no further effort to please.

Count Orlanov, however, was exerting himself in the most gracious way to gain her good will, and she was flattered. "Tell me, Miss Dalrymple," he said once they were settled, "are all English women as delightful as you?"

"Alas, in the opinion of many I am surpassed by a good number of other English women."

"That is not possible, surely," said the count leaning toward her. "I cannot imagine there are many woman your equal, and surely there are none superior. If that were so it would place an intolerable strain on your men, for how could they possibly deserve such paragons?"

"Most men, I believe, have no trouble at all feeling they deserve much better than they receive."

"I am sure you are not speaking from experience, but from hearsay, for no man who had been graced with your attentions could possibly aspire to more."

Chastity laughed. "You are quite right. I am not speaking from experience, but from observation, which is a much safer route to knowledge, I believe."

"Safer, perhaps, but not nearly so amusing," said Count Orlanov. Though he dropped his voice a bare half-note it was sufficient to signal that in his mind the conversation was assuming more significance.

"As to that, sir," she said lightly, "I shall have to rely upon your word."

"You can rely absolutely upon my word—and upon me," he said, increasing his ardor by another notch. It seemed to Chastity they had progressed quite far enough in this direction.

"Well," she said brightly, "you are the first person I have ever met from Russia. Is your home in Saint Petersburg also?"

"Yes. That is where I was born and educated. But now I have stepped out into the greater world of Europe."

"You have left Russia for good?"

"That depends," said Count Orlanov, his blue eyes piercing again, "upon whether something or someone detains me."

"For the moment, I gather, you are being detained in England by Lady Grasset," said Chastity. She had been emboldened by the easy tone of their exchange to slake her curiosity.

Count Orlanov's expression shifted slightly toward wariness. "I have been assigned to be Lady Grasset's escort."

"Are all single women in Russia so fortunate as to have escorts assigned them? What a pleasant custom. It quite does away with the necessity for husbands."

"Surely not, Miss Dalrymple. Are you saying that in England the husbands only escort their wives, while all other marital functions are assigned elsewhere, such as to lovers, perhaps?"

Chastity found the comment bold. She had, she realized, been led out of her depth. She stiffened and her smile froze as she began to paddle back toward the shore. "What an interesting place Russia must be, and how I should like to hear more about it. But for the present I fear I must search out my aunt who will be wondering what has become of me." She rose.

Count Orlanov rose also, and placed a gently restraining hand on her arm. "I have offended you. I apologize. You are the first English woman I have had a discussion with, and I was not aware of having said something amiss."

Chastity felt priggish, and was embarrassed that her reaction had been so provincial. She smiled ruefully at Count Orlanov and said, "You have not offended me at all, sir. On the contrary, I have been delighted to chat with you. But I really must return to my aunt now." Her smile was warm.

"There you are!" said Lady Grasset, playfully chiding. "Hiding from the rest of the merrymakers." She was accompanied by a very solemn Charles Techett.

Chastity was not sure whether it was she or Count Orlanov being addressed, but she started guiltily. "We have just been discussing Saint Petersburg," she said, and was aware the remark sounded lame.

"There is no one who can tell you more about the subject," said Lady Grasset brightly, "or who can make it more interesting." To Count Orlanov, who stood at attention, she said, "You have promised me a dance, Peter, and I have quite bored poor Mr. Techett with my clumsiness, so he won't ever lead me toward the floor again." She smiled at Chastity. "I must steal him away, or I shall be forced to sit with the chaperones. Will you excuse us?"

"Certainly," said Chastity as Lady Grasset lifted a fleshy arm toward Count Orlanov.

He bowed to Chastity and said, "It has been a pleasure, Miss Dalrymple, one I will not allow to end here." He led Lady Grasset away, leaving Chastity standing near a frozen faced Charles Techett.

The silence was strained, and Chastity was annoyed she should feel guilty about such an innocent situation. It was true the conversation had strayed toward impropriety, but it had been retrieved in time, and furthermore Charles had not heard it. Why, then, was he looking so disapproving, and why did she feel she had done something wrong?

"Are you enjoying the ball, Mr. Techett?" she asked.

"Yes. It is very amusing," said Charles flatly.

"So far I have only danced once, but I found the orchestra to be very fine," said Chastity.

Charles nodded curtly.

"Do you know where I might find my aunt?" asked Chastity after a pause.

"Yes. She asked me to see what had become of you," said Charles coldly, and gave her a rapid look in which she caught censure.

"Then let us not disturb her further by making her continue to wonder," said Chastity shortly. "Please lead me to her."

Silently he proffered his arm, and silently she took it. Both stared straight ahead, expressionless and stiff. Chastity could not fathom the reasons for Charles's glacial aloofness, but she decided that if she could not dissolve it, she could, at least, surpass it. They marched through the guests like two executioners headed for the scaffold. Grimly they bore down upon Lady Trentower, herself hardly a model of jollity.

"So you've decided to return to the ball," said the old woman with ill humor.

Chastity was truly astonished at this line of attack, and stared for an instant at her aunt before answering, "I have never left the ball."

Charles excused himself; neither Chastity nor Lady Trentower paid him more than a passing nod in acknowledgment.

"You can hardly be said to have partaken of the festivities, closeted as you were for so long a time with that Russian," said Lady Trentower, sitting stiffly in her chair and glaring at Chastity. "If you have no consideration for your own reputation, you might at least have considered mine."

Chastity was dumbfounded. That her innocent interlude with Count Orlanov could have caused such an uproar never occurred to her. She basked in regard at Grangeford, where she could do no wrong, where she could remain alone in a room with any gentleman and emerge with reputation unscathed; that a few minutes sitting in full view of a roomful of strangers could lead her aunt to such excessively censurious remarks at first confused rather than angered her. This was London, where the manners were supposedly freer and more easygoing than in the counties.

"Count Orlanov and I can hardly be said to have been closeted. There was no door, nor even curtain separating us from the other guests," said Chastity coldly. "Nor can our conversation have lasted more than a few moments. You are exaggerating."

"I should have thought," said Lady Trentower,

still fuming, "that at twenty-seven years of age you would have learned the rudiments of propriety. Though you are no longer young, you are still unmarried, and unmarried girls do not go off with young men and sit with them intimately. It was shocking, sitting there with your heads together."

"Our heads were not together. If you think you saw such a thing your eyes have deceived you. Furthermore, you yourself have left me alone with Mr. Techett."

"I did not have to rely upon my eyes. Several of my most trusted friends have told me what they saw. When *I* left you alone with Charles I did so in such a way that no one would know. I did not install you in an alcove in front of all society. I have rarely been so mortified. First I am called sister by that adventuress, and now my niece takes it into her head to beguile the woman's lover. One would think our family had tainted blood."

"Lover?" said Chastity. "Count Orlanov is Lady Grasset's lover? How do you know that?"

"All society knows it. Just look at them. What else could he be? But that's beside the point. Even if he were her brother, or her father, it still would not be proper to lure him into a niche and stay with him."

"You insult me, ma'am, and I shall not put up with it," said Chastity evenly. "There was no impropriety in my behavior, nor has there ever been. I have never lured any man, and for you to assert I have merely displays your ill-humor toward me."

Lady Trentower softened her attitude somewhat, whether in contrition for having been so harsh, or in fear of creating a scene was not clear.

"It is possible," she said grudgingly, "that you acted innocently. But it is the behavior, not the motives, by which you are judged in society. You have flouted one of society's rules. You cannot do that very often if you intend to snare a husband."

"I have no wish to 'snare' a husband. I am not here on a hunt, contrary to what you may believe," said Chastity furiously, keeping her voice low and controlled.

As though to discourage an insect, Lady Trentower waved her hand at Chastity's remark. "Persist in this fiction if you wish. But you know, as do I, that you have no other reason for being here. You will return to Kent empty-handed unless you watch your step."

Chastity was angry and humiliated, all the more so because she really did want a husband. This admission to her aunt, however, would render her too vulnerable; so even though she was honest enough with herself, she was prevented from being as open as her nature dictated, and she felt fraudulent. She loathed acting naive when she was nothing of the sort.

"At the moment," she said proudly, "I shall return to your home. You have succeeded in spoiling the ball for me."

"And I shall leave also," said Lady Trentower, rising majestically, "for you have quite wrecked *my* pleasure."

"Dear sister," said Lady Grasset, who swooped down at them from the dance floor, still on the arm of Count Orlanov, "you have not once danced. Peter, you must dance with Lady Trentower," she said imperiously, though playfully.

Count Orlanov bowed and would have stepped

forward had Lady Trentower not stiffened and said, "I have not danced for years, madame, and will not do so now." She looked annoyed. "In fact, we are just leaving, as soon as we can find Mr. Techett."

"Surely," said Lady Grasset, "you will not leave so soon? I can't allow it. You are not only depriving us of your company but are enticing Mr. Techett to go with you." She pouted prettily, as a much younger girl might have done.

Charles Techett came to the little group, still solemn and unbending, and Lady Grasset turned to him, her fat face dimpled with mock chagrin. "You are being led away, sir. You are deserting the ball."

He looked from her to Chastity, and then to Lady Trentower, who said testily, "There is no need for you to leave at all, Charles, if you will simply give us the use of your carriage. Both my niece and I are feeling indisposed."

"I hope," said Lady Grasset, "it is nothing that you have eaten or drunk here that has made you ill? I could never forgive myself if I had brought harm to my dear sister and niece."

Charles, to both Lady Trentower and Chastity, said, "I am sorry you are not well. Of course you may take the carriage." Turning full to Chastity he added, "I regret we have not had our dance." He was formal and unsmiling.

Chastity barely nodded. Count Orlanov suddenly left Lady Grasset's side and took Chastity's hand. "Miss Dalrymple, I shall see you again, and soon," he said intensely, then stepped back. He was the only one in the little group whose behavior seemed unconstrained. She smiled at him. "It will be a pleasure, sir," she said.

"Let us be going," said Lady Trentower, exasperated. She marched from the ballroom, and Chastity, careful to remain erect and to walk casually as though she were strolling from the ball rather than being routed from a scene of embarrassment, followed.

Chapter Four

Chastity awoke the next morning despondent. Images of the evening before swam through her head as she stretched: herself, exquisite in white muslin; Charles Techett's admiring appraisal; Count Orlanov's piercing gaze as he bent over her; Lady Grasset's huge bosom set off by diamonds and black satin; Lady Trentower's glum visage on the ride back from the ball.

She sighed and rang for tea. Perhaps, she thought, she should return to Grangeford. Perhaps she should resign herself to the role of the maiden daughter who stays at home to look after an aging parent—no matter that her father could not care less whether she stayed or married, so long as she left him to the pursuit of his innocent habits. Perhaps that would be easier.

The sudden memory of how Count Orlanov's arm felt around her waist and the sparkle of Charles Techett's eyes as they probed hers erased that train of thought, and she knew that though she might end up as a maiden daughter, it would be against her will. Flitting through her mind, like some ominous bird, had been the idea of packing up and leaving London, returning to Grangeford where she would not be bothered by the peculiar delicacy of her cantankerous aunt. But she feared that such an escape would doom her to solitude. With a grim sigh she burrowed into her bed and resolved to go through the season, and come out of it with a husband.

With her morning tea came a note. She inspected the square, the seal of which was indistinct, with anticipation. Very likely, she thought, it came from Charles Techett, and contained an explanation for his singularly dour behavior toward her. Possibly it was an apology. She lingered over that image for a few seconds before leaping to an equally, maybe even more so, delicious fantasy: The note was from Count Orlanov and was an avowal of some kind. At the very least it was an announcement of his intention to visit her.

She smiled wryly. She was always most susceptible when she had just awakened, her imagination most vulnerable. She knew very well that any such highly romantic developments were implausible, even illogical, yet she hoped nonetheless that she had surmised correctly or at least had come close to divining the contents.

With a sigh, half-resigned and half-anticipatory, she broke the seal, and after a few seconds of rapidly running her eye over the lines and signature, she sighed more deeply and fell against the pillows hopelessly. Never, she thought, never could one foretell all the things that could go wrong in one's life. She lifted the note again and read:

Dear Miss Dalrymple,
Business has brought me to London, and though I was loathe to leave Harrowgate, I came with a joyful heart because I knew this great city contained one whose welfare I

cherish above all others, viz., you. I beg leave
to call upon you at two o'clock this afternoon.

> Your obedient and ever
> faithful servant,
>
> Joseph Brockton, Esq.

If someone had asked her who she would be least happy to see she would have named Joseph Brockton, if she had thought of him at all. There was no animosity, no hostility in the notice she gave him, there was simply a dreary grayness surrounding his person in her mind's eye. She reflected that some girls might be happy to have a suitor who was unshakably devoted, particularly one who would be considered a creditable catch by almost anyone who was interested in such matters. She was not. Even though just moments before she had resolved—with all the grim determination at her command—to catch a husband before the season was out, she now amended her resolution to mean that she would catch a husband who was a man of dash. Joseph Brockton, she thought, with a weary shake of the head, did not even begin to fill that bill.

She glumly rose from her bed and began her toilet. What she could rely upon, she reflected sourly, was that Joseph Brockton was most assuredly a man of his word, and that if he said he would call at two o'clock, he was certain to be in the drawing room precisely at that hour. She would, of course, have to receive him. In addition, she would have to present him to her aunt, and heaven only knew what unpleasantness that encounter would produce.

After she was dressed she descended to the dining room where she found Lady Trentower in excellent spirits eating breakfast with a hearty appetite.

"Good morning," she greeted Chastity cheerfully from behind a plate loaded with eggs, beef and a thick slab of bread. "I trust you slept well."

Lady Trentower had the ability to begin each day anew, accumulating and dispersing her dissatisfaction with people and events as they came up. She always appeared to hail the morning with a clean slate. On this morning she apparently had no recollection of the unpleasantness that had marred the parting with her niece the night before. Chastity was more retentive, and was unable to disguise her ill-feeling.

"Very well," she said coolly, and selected a spoonful of eggs and a small biscuit from the sideboard.

"Splendid," said Lady Trentower. "There's nothing like a ball to tire one out and assure a good night's rest." She appeared unaware of the irony in her remark. Chastity merely glanced at her with veiled animosity, before saying, "I received a note from a gentleman who is a neighbor of ours in Kent. He is in London for business, and has written to say he will call this afternoon."

Lady Trentower was instantly alert. She raised her head, her eyes lively with curiosity, and said, "I was not aware that you had any gentlemen friends near you."

"There are many gentlemen in our vicinity,"

said Chastity testily, "and this is merely one who happens to be in London."

"Is he unattached?" asked Lady Trentower.

"He is unmarried, yes," said Chastity shortly.

"What is his age?"

"I do not know."

"Come, come," said Lady Trentower briskly. "You are not stupid, you can arrive at some estimate. Is he infirm, ancient, doubled over with age? Or is he dewy cheeked, and still lisping with youth? Or is he in the prime of life?"

"I surmise he is in his late thirties."

"A perfect age for a husband!" said Lady Trentower.

Chastity, as so often happened when she was with her aunt, set her mouth and stared straight ahead, attempting to avoid the conversational nets the old woman was casting. As happened just as frequently, Lady Trentower would have none of it.

"Why did you come gallivanting to London when you had likely quarry in your own garden?"

"Mr. Brockton is not quarry. He is a gentleman who is a neighbor."

"Ah-ha-ha," said Lady Trentower, her eyes narrowed astutely. "I begin to comprehend. We have set our cap for Mr. Brockton, and he has proven elusive. He did not rise to the bait in our traps. He was getting away, so we came to London to create the absence that makes the heart grow fonder." Lady Trentower nodded her head roguishly as she spoke, and winked conspiratorially.

Chastity was appalled at this misinterpretation. At the same time she refused to lower herself to the point of making a defense of her behavior and setting her aunt straight. She restricted herself to a curt disclaimer.

"You are quite mistaken," she said coldly.

"My dear child, I am a woman of the world. I have seen a great deal, and I assure you, I know all there is to know about husband hunting. You may believe that I am mistaken, but I am not. Rely upon me, child. I shall help you snare your Mr. Brockton."

"I beg you to do nothing of the sort," said Chastity hotly, her veneer scratched by this new threat.

Lady Trentower shook her finger playfully. "Sly little puss! I am beginning to understand my niece. She says one thing and means another. She tries to hide her thoughts from her old aunt. My dear child, you have nothing to be ashamed of. Husband hunting is a pastime that is as honorable as any other type of hunting, and is certainly more worthwhile than most. Don't be embarrassed. Am I not a woman—and your aunt?" Lady Trentower was enjoying herself hugely. She was, Chastity reflected, acting out a role, that of a woman of the world as well as a concerned relative, and for the moment nothing could dampen her fantasy. Chastity sat at the table, looking glumly at her plate while her aunt rambled on, expatiating on what her niece should wear, how she should greet her visitor ("Not too eager, but not too distant.") and how she would arrange for them to be alone once he arrived. Finally Chastity could bear no more.

"Aunt," she said sternly, "you are so completely mistaken in your interpretation of this visit that I cannot permit this discussion to continue."

Her tone of voice pulled Lady Trentower up and

put a restraint on her enthusiasm. "In what way am I mistaken?" she asked peevishly.

"Mr. Brockton would like my hand in marriage. I do not wish it."

"Then you are a foolish girl," said Lady Trentower decisively.

"I remind you, aunt, that you do not know the gentleman, have never even heard his name before this morning."

"There is such a thing as intuition," said Lady Trentower. "I *feel* this gentleman should be your husband."

Chastity's face grew red with anger, but she said nothing for a few seconds. Then, calmly, she rose and quietly said, "You are mistaken. I have nothing more to say on the subject. I shall receive Mr. Brockton for politeness' sake when he calls. You are welcome to meet him if you wish." Mustering a show of serenity she glided from the room, leaving a disgruntled Lady Trentower behind her.

True to his word and character Joseph Brockton arrived on the dot of two o'clock. If only, Chastity mused, punctuality could be transmuted into something more interesting, Mr. Brockton might have possibilities. She descended with an expression of tolerant good will, and entered the drawing room with calculated graciousness.

Joseph Brockton had not changed during the months she had been absent. He was still tall, stocky, a little red in the face, neat. His clothes did not look provincial, though they were by no means dandified. He could have passed on the street for any London gentleman of substance. "My dear Miss Dalrymple," he said as she entered.

He crossed and took her hand in his with warmth. "What a pleasure it gives me to see you again."

"How kind of you to call," said Chastity with a polite but perfunctory smile. "I hope you had a pleasant journey."

"The journey was agreeable as such things can be, and my stay, which is just beginning with this visit, augurs very well indeed."

She smiled and indicated a chair. Just as they settled stiffly into positions facing each other Lady Trentower gaily entered the drawing room.

"Oh, there you are," she said to Chastity, as though she had been searching for her high and low. "But do excuse me! You have a visitor!" With a charming smile she turned to Mr. Brockton who had risen.

Drily Chastity introduced them. Mr. Brockton bowed gravely as he took Lady Trentower's hand and she warbled, "Where are you visiting from?"

"Harrowgate, in Kent, ma'am."

"Ah, then, you must be neighbors!" said Lady Trentower, gesturing toward Chastity, and in a tone that indicated she was delighted at this discovery. Chastity grudgingly admired her aunt's display of agreeableness. "Is Harrowgate the name of your little village?"

"No, ma'am, it is what my estate is called."

"What a pretty name! An estate. Is it near Grangeford?"

"Barely twenty miles distant, ma'am," said Mr. Brockton, responding to Lady Trentower's catechizing with deference.

Lady Trentower glanced triumphantly at Chastity. It was obvious that in her own mind she took credit for flushing this eminently suitable gentleman from his cover for her niece's inspection.

"How pleasant it must be to have such neighbors," she continued brightly, smiling almost coquettishly at Mr. Brockton who was basking in her attention.

During their exchange Chastity sat with a stony and noncommittal smile. She wondered what she could say to defuse her aunt's obvious matchmaking, which would, she feared, give rise to unfounded expectations on Mr. Brockton's part. Just as she was about to make some general remark, the footman announced Lady Grasset and Count Orlanov.

As on her previous visit, Lady Grasset did not wait to receive an invitation to enter, but rather rushed into the drawing room at full tilt. Count Orlanov followed at a more sedate pace.

"Dearest sister," said Lady Grasset to Lady Trentower, whose expression recalled frost nipping an orchard of apple blossoms, "I could hardly sleep all night, what with worrying about your health. And yours, also, dear niece," she added to Chastity. Returning to Lady Trentower: "I hope your malaise has disappeared. I could not forgive myself if something at our little fete was the cause of it."

"I am quite well, madame," said Lady Trentower chillingly.

"Heavens be praised," said Lady Grasset fervently, raising her eyes and placing her hand on her enormous bosom, as though to quiet her palpitating heart. "The Grand Duchess will be so pleased. She, also, was extremely worried." She smiled brilliantly at Mr. Brockton who had risen, and said, "Health is so important, don't you think?"

"I certainly agree, ma'am," said Mr. Brockton gravely.

"I was so worried about my dear sister," Lady Grasset continued, "that I had to rush over immediately upon rising."

Mr. Brockton said to Lady Trentower, "You are fortunate to have such a caring sister, ma'am."

"We are not really sisters," said Lady Trentower grimly. "This is Lady Grasset, the wife of my brother." She added, as if the information would serve to make the relationship even more remote, "My brother is deceased." She looked disapprovingly at Count Orlanov for a few seconds, and then presented him.

He was splendid again in spotless white uniform trimmed with gold braid, and carrying the casque with its spurt of crimson feathers. He bowed to Mr. Brockton from the waist, but said nothing.

"You, sir," said Lady Grasset to Mr. Brockton as she settled on one of the gilt chairs she made look perilously fragile, "why weren't you at our ball last evening? Don't pretend you were," she hastened to add, raising a fat arm in a graceful gesture of playful command, "for certainly I would have seen you had you been there."

"Mr. Brockton has just arrived in London," said Lady Trentower in a proprietorial fashion. "He has come to visit Miss Dalrymple," she added significantly.

"Fortunate niece," said Lady Grasset turning a brilliant smile on Chastity.

Mr. Brockton, accustomed to crossing t's and

dotting i's, was unable to leave any loose ends in the conversation. "Ball?" he inquired judiciously. "I heard of no ball."

"That is only because you were not yet in London," said Lady Grasset, leaning toward him, and touching him lightly on the arm with her fan. "I assure you, that had I known of the existence of such a charming gentleman I should not have let the opportunity pass to invite him to meet the Grand Duchess Catherine."

"Of Russia?" said Mr. Brockton, startled out of his usual imperturbability.

"My dearest friend," said Lady Grasset demurely. Looking quickly at Lady Trentower, she added, "Or, rather, one of my dearest friends."

This promotion from sister to dearest friend sat badly with Lady Trentower, and caused her to look darkly around her, searching vainly for some means to dissolve the gathering.

"I am indeed sorry to have missed such an opportunity," said Mr. Brockton. His admiration for Lady Grasset visibly increased.

Chastity was paying hardly any attention to the undercurrents swirling around her, for she had engaged Count Orlanov's eye, and he, encouraged, had moved to her side.

"I regretted your early departure last night," he said softly. "I could not help feeling that in some way I did not understand, I had contributed to your difficulties." He looked so fixedly into her eyes that she had to drop them.

"I appreciate your concern, sir, but I assure you your only contribution was to my enjoyment of the ball," said Chastity, equally softly. They formed a little pocket of conspiratorial quiet in the drawing room.

Count Orlanov continued looking at her intently, his blue eyes roving over her face as if searching for a signal. Lowering his voice almost to a whisper and leaning a fraction closer he said, "If we were alone I would seize your hand and kiss it."

Chastity caught her breath. It was not the threat of having her hand kissed that stunned her, but the passion that informed the statement. "I...think, sir, that..."

"You think I go too far. I do. I am a blackguard, made reckless by proximity to you. I cannot act, I cannot touch—all I am allowed are a few words, and they are inadequate to express my longing for you." His voice was a whisper, and his expression was carefully guarded. No one within the drawing room could have divined the intent of his remarks by looking at him.

Chastity wondered whether she should terminate this interview by rising to her feet. Perhaps she should publicly chide the man? By sitting there was she not a party to his declaration, did that not constitute an acceptance of it? She glanced hastily around the room. No one was looking their way. The evening before when Count Orlanov had barely veered toward the outer limits of conventionality she had quelled his ardor. Now he had leaped across the line into the nearest thing to abandon she had ever witnessed, and she continued sitting silently as though she were accustomed to hearing such declarations every day of her life. She breathed deeply, but very quietly, several times, before saying, "Evidently, sir, by some action or gesture or word I have misled you into thinking you have permission to speak so intimately to me. You do not." Her voice, pitched as low as his, sounded as though she were whispering a secret.

"You have done nothing reprehensible. You are incapable of such action. It is I who am to blame, for I have never before encountered such perfection. The experience has unhinged me and made me act like a villain. Forgive me, but pity me also, and do not turn me away." As before, Count Orlanov retained his facade of polite attention, and the fierce and astonishing words were delivered in a subdued monotone. These circumstances, added to his extraordinary handsomeness, left Chastity disoriented. She mustered every bit of her control to appear as indifferent as he; but this was just a delaying tactic, for she could not decide whether to denounce the count, tacitly accept his declaration or actively dissuade him from pursuing the subject. In truth she wanted to follow all three courses. On the rock of such disparate alternatives she sat as still as a chameleon.

"India!" said a thrilled Lady Grasset, breaking into Chastity's dilemma, "imagine that! Peter, this gentleman comes from India!"

Count Orlanov bowed in acknowledgment of the fact and Mr. Brockton, preening himself, returned the bow. To Lady Grasset he said, "It has been some time since I was there, ma'am. I did not just arrive."

"Even so," said Lady Grasset, determined to be impressed, "such a great distance! It makes our little journey from Russia seem like the merest jaunt." She turned to Lady Trentower. "Travel is the best educator of all, don't you think, sister?"

Lady Trentower glowered. "I have never felt the need to leave England," she said with asperity, "and I feel quite adequately educated."

"Of course," Lady Grasset hastened to say, "there is such a thing as natural intelligence. How I admire it. There are those of us, however, who have to work for our information." She smiled at Mr. Brockton, who had fallen under her spell.

Lady Trentower stirred and seemed inclined to deliver her own opinion on natural intelligence when her footman quietly announced Charles Techett.

"Now, my dear sister," said Lady Grasset, delighted, "you can boast the presence of two of the most fascinating men in London." She smiled significantly at Mr. Brockton just as Charles Techett entered the room. Count Orlanov, who apparently was not included in Lady Grasset's inventory of fascinating men, sat impassively.

Charles was surprised by the number of guests. He stiffly acknowledged the introduction to Mr. Brockton after having greeted the other members of the party, and then took his seat and looked around appraisingly. "I trust you are feeling better, ma'am," he said judiciously to Lady Trentower, and nodded to Chastity to show he included her in his query.

Lady Trentower bridled. "I have never felt better in my life. For the past several years I have enjoyed only the most exemplary health." She had completely forgotten her ostensible reason for leaving the ball the evening before, and was vexed at the inexplicable attention paid her health by Lady Grasset and now Charles.

"I am delighted to hear it," said Charles, showing no disposition to pursue the subject.

Lady Grasset beamed at him. "Dear Charles, so thoughtful." Looking around she exclaimed, "What a delightful little band we are—how kind and sparkling! It was well worth a trip to London just to be able to witness such an assembly." She was quite seduced by her observation, and particularly embraced Charles and Mr. Brockton with her smile.

Lady Trentower was growing stiffer and glummer by the minute. She inspected her guests with marked distaste. Her annoyance was exacerbated by the fact that no one paid any attention to it; rather, Lady Grasset had so competently assumed the responsibility for the conversation that Lady Trentower found herself superfluous in her own drawing room.

Chastity, after she had reassured herself that no one had noticed her exchange with Count Orlanov, began to observe the peculiar turn events were taking: Mr. Brockton was now completely under the spell of Lady Grasset, and hardly even glanced her way. Charles Techett, who she assumed had come to call on her, was becoming ensnared in the same toils. Lady Grasset was appropriating her suitors.

It was true she had long since crossed Mr. Brockton off her list of possibilities, so in theory it would be surly of her to object to his sudden switch of allegiance. Yet her amour propre was shaken as she watched Lady Grasset reel him into her sphere with hardly a flick of the wrist. Chastity would have preferred at least a token show of loyalty on his part.

As for Charles Techett, she had by no means forsworn that gentleman's attentions, and his defection was considerably more disturbing. She watched him covertly as he leaned toward the enormous Lady Grasset, vying with Mr. Brockton for her attention. For a few moments she all but forgot the silent but intense presence of Count Orlanov who continued to sit at her side. Suddenly she was startled to hear him whisper in her ear.

"When can we meet alone?"

"I . . . why, that is . . ."

"I know my request is bold. Forward, even. But please honor it."

"I'm afraid that a meeting, sir . . ."

"I have only touched you once, at the ball last night. Can I not feel your flesh in some other circumstance than on the ballroom floor?"

"Sir!" she whispered sternly. "You forget yourself!" She was so truly shocked that she allowed the volume of her voice to exceed the level of conversation around her, and her exclamation brought a sudden surprised lull to the assembly as all turned to look at her. She blushed brightly, but otherwise maintained her composure, and returned their stares with insouciance. It is, however, impossible to convince a group of people that nothing untoward has happened when one is glowing bright red from the neck up.

"Whatever is the problem?" asked Lady Trentower, looking at her niece with alarm.

"My dear," chimed in Lady Grasset, "have you swallowed something awry?"

With as much calm as she could muster Chastity discouraged their questions by stating, "Something has caught in my throat. Please excuse me." She rose and would have left the room, had not Lady Grasset also jumped to her feet, declaring, "It is time we left also, for I don't think my dear niece has quite recovered from her indisposition of last evening." She threw Chastity an ostentatiously concerned look. Her remark and action brought all the men to their feet, and suddenly, in the grip of a force beyond their control, both Mr. Brockton and Charles Techett were declaring that they, also, must be leaving. "In that case," said Lady Grasset, "perhaps you will both be kind enough to accompany me on my rounds? I have some visits to pay—duty visits for the Grand Duchess—and how light the burden will be if I am accompanied by two such gallant cavaliers."

Both men agreed with alacrity, and within a few seconds Lady Grasset had sailed from the room like a frigate towing three prizes behind her. With what seemed almost magical suddenness, Lady Trentower and Chastity found themselves alone in the drawing room.

Chapter Five

Lady Trentower was fit to be tied. She sputtered. "Well... And that... What..." Collecting herself she glared at Chastity and demanded, "What do you think of your other aunt now? That is what comes of being kind to guttersnipes. You let them into your home, you treat them with consideration, and they sink their fangs into your bosom at the first opportunity." Her outrage was that of one who has been betrayed and deceived; she had conveniently forgotten, in order to bolster her indignation, that from the first news of her sister-in-law's arrival she had forseen only the direst consequences. "Why, that woman has swooped through my drawing room like a pirate, snatching my very guests from under my nose!"

Chastity felt that if anyone had been deprived of guests it was herself. Mr. Brockton had, she presumed, some to see her, and Charles Techett had evinced interest of a more than merely social sort in her presence. Count Orlanov had made the purpose of his visit quite clear, to her, if not to the gathering at large. These were the three gentlemen that Lady Grasset had made off with, and by doing so had left Chastity thoroughly confounded. How was she to react? Was she to regard, suddenly, her younger aunt as her rival? Was, in fact, Lady Grasset out to snatch her suitors—and what a meager lot they were—from her grasp? If this indeed was the case, then Chastity had been thrust into an arena where she was ill-prepared for combat. She had never competed for the attention of gentlemen before; rather, she had always been sought after, and by men whose ardor was not distracted by any other female.

She found the possibility she might be pushed into a struggle for suitors highly distasteful. Her first reaction was that she would simply withdraw and not deign to resort to wiles. But then, seeping into consciousness came the dreary reality of her situation: she was an unmarried girl who, she had to avow, wished to alter her situation by the addition of a spouse. If such an alteration could be effected only by resorting to vigorous measures, well, then, so be it. Her deep sigh was misinterpreted by her aunt as resignation.

"So," said Lady Trentower, "you're just going to sit there feeling sorry for yourself. There is no stamina in your generation. When I was your age, of course, I had already been married for ten years, but believe me, if I had by some bizarre set of circumstances found myself in an unmarried state by the time I was twenty-seven years old, I would have moved heaven and earth to change the fact. I would have succeeded, too."

"Do be quiet," said Chastity. Lady Trentower's jaw dropped and she stared at her niece with disbelief. Chastity had been startled by her own outburst; she had not yet realized the extent to which she had been vexed by Lady Grasset's absconding with the three males in her life, and did not understand that this salvo fired at her older aunt was a misdirected attempt to riddle her younger one. She immediately regretted her loss of control, but not to the extent of apologizing. Instead, she announced, "I am going to my room to rest." She stalked out, leaving Lady Trentower staring after her with a very put-upon expression.

Once in her room, Chastity admitted she had no idea how to circumvent Lady Grasset's maneuvers. She began to doubt that what she had witnessed had been a definite plan on the part of her enormous younger aunt; might not the three gentlemen have been swept away by accident? Perhaps Lady Grasset was acting without any guile at all, in the simple way a sudden storm comes sweeping through a garden, flattening all the blossoms in its path; in such an event one would be foolish to chide nature for destructive behavior.

After reliving those brief moments during which Lady Grasset gathered up the men around her and led them off, however, she reflected that no operation that succeeded so well could have been accidental. No, Lady Grasset was a schemer.

One splinter of comfort was the memory of her whispered exchange with Count Orlanov. That proved her rival (she could think of her only as such) was not invincible. If Count Orlanov had been, or still was, Lady Grasset's lover, then Chastity could boast—providing she ever sank to that level, which she was determined not to do—that she had won a rather significant victory herself. Then, however, she wondered whether her *sotto voce* conversation with the count had been leading to an honorable declaration on his part or to an attempt at a sordid liaison. As she reviewed the count's behavior, his insistence and his secretiveness, she had to admit that to an impartial observer both possibilities were equally weighted. At the time she had given him the benefit of the doubt—but this was more because her own experience as the recipient of such bold attentions was limited. She had never, during her other courtships, been subjected to any but the most upright advances. Now, she wondered whether she would even recognize a dishonorable one. She mulled over the count's words and gestures, and finally decided that surely all had been marshaled with marriage in view. He was, certainly, an exotic creature, both in appearance and provenance, so it was not possible for her to judge his motives with any degree of sureness. She relied on her intuition.

Having come to the conclusion that Count Orlanov was wooing her with matrimony as his object, she had to ponder whether she would accept him if he ever put the question squarely to her. She was confused, for in a very short while he had pushed his attentions beyond the borders of decorum set by her other suitors. Also, she was wary of his looks; he was so handsome that she feared she would slant any interpretation of his actions in his favor if at all possible. What woman would not bend her judgment if by doing so she could justify encouraging the attentions of such a splendid-looking creature? As for whether she would acquiesce if all her doubts were overcome—well, she would have to wait and see what developed.

That, in fact, was the most vexing part of her situation; she would have to wait patiently in Lady Trentower's drawing room for events to come to her. She had not the excuse of a connection with

Russian royalty to be out and about in society. Lady Grasset, as handmaiden to the Grand Duchess Catherine, could stalk any prey she chose. Certainly she was using her *laisser aller* without stint, to judge by the accounts appearing in the journals over the next few days. Lady Grasset, as the only Englishwoman in the Russian entourage received almost as much attention as the Grand Duchess herself; her clothes were remarked, as were her new acquaintances, and her general comings and goings. The only thing that was not generally investigated, according to a captious Lady Trentower, were the woman's antecedents. "Mercifully for her, I should say," she added.

Grand Duchess Catherine was inspiring a spate of stories and gossip that, little by little, began to reflect a rather unpleasant light upon her. She had, for instance, roundly snubbed the Prince Regent by refusing his purely formal invitation to dinner at Carlton House, and then by loudly asserting to anyone within earshot that she found him gross, ill-mannered and generally distasteful. As it happened the Prince Regent was passing through a period of frightful unpopularity—there was even talk of forcing him to abdicate—and possibly the Grand Duchess thought that since his own subjects did not seem to like him very much, she would endear herself to the populace by giving voice to their discontent. What she foolishly failed to realize (if this was her scheme) was that most Englishmen thoroughly enjoyed lambasting their own sovereign, whether through the cruel drawings of Gillray in the journals or in the more direct way of shouted insults as the hapless man rode through the streets from palace to Parliament;

however, they resented with enormous gusto any foreign criticism, regardless of how nearly it coincided with their own views. So while the Grand Duchess Catherine was merrily and spitefully airing her opinions about "Fat George," as she called him, she was at the same time undermining the goodwill the city had borne her upon arrival. Surely someone in her entourage must have pointed this out; certainly there were references to her indiscretion in the press. Grand Duchess Catherine, however, was not accustomed to tailor her behavior to suit a critical press (there was no such thing in Russia) or to quell admonitions from her courtiers. Finally, she became so rambunctious and outspoken that Count Leiven, the Russian ambassador to England, threatened to resign if she would not curtail her animosity towards the British sovereign. He contended that he could not maintain diplomatic ties between his country and England when the sister of his Tsar was gleefully insulting her host at every chance. Rumor had it that this rebuke caused a great deal of sulking, and even inspired threats to leave the country immediately. This was an alternative that no one, aristocrat or plebian, wished, for it was common knowledge that the Grand Duchess was a harbinger of her brother the Tsar. Though she might be an unpleasant guest, everyone was willing to put up with her for the privilege of seeing and cheering Tsar Alexander, the hero who had fought and defeated that scourge of Europe and threat to Britain, Napoleon. It was feared that if the Tsar's favorite sister decamped, the hero himself would not grace the nation's shores. So a certain amount of grudging official tolerance was extended to Catherine.

It was a curious comment upon society that though any well-placed individual who was queried about the Grand Duchess's behavior would roundly denounce it, that same individual would scramble like a caged rodent to meet the lady if the opportunity loomed even faintly on his or her horizon. In short, the Grand Duchess was politically and popularly decried, but was socially the most desirable pinnacle that could be attained during the London spring of 1814.

According to the journals, Lady Grasset blithely went her rounds, which were daily increasing in size and importance; seemingly she was unaware of the conflict her patroness inspired, much as a plump and delectable raisin is probably impervious to the pudding in which it finds itself. Everyone received her; almost everyone liked her. She was a novelty, an original, an unknown. Though her past was no secret, it was tactfully overlooked; there was not one mention of her former career or liaisons in the gazettes.

Such reticence did not pertain in Lady Trentower's drawing room when she was alone with Chastity; then, no excoriation was too severe for her sister-in-law. Even that redoubtable dowager, however, curbed her tongue when she was visited by or went visiting with her peers, for she did not have the courage to vilify someone so universally approved. After one of these visits, though, where Lady Trentower had sat with a forced smile while hearing an account of Lady Grasset's latest triumph, an invitation to Carlton House to meet the Prince Regent, she had muttered through clenched teeth, "When will they see through the woman? Am I the only sane person left in London? Why is it so clear to me, and not to them, that she is a guttersnipe in finery, aping her betters?"

Chastity, to whom this complaint was uttered, said nothing. Nor did she indicate by attitude or expression that she disagreed with her aunt, as she probably would have only a few days before. She was beginning to regard Lady Grasset as a very distinct danger to her matrimonial aspirations, and as such she could not bring herself to contradict even the most far-fetched and venomous of Lady Trentower's denunciations. She was jealous. This was a new and painful facet of her character, for never before had she suffered the pangs that are flushed to the surface when someone else threatens our self-esteem by acquiring an individual we thought was committed to us. At Grangeford, Chastity had always been the one who was desired and sought after; as such she had controlled all courtships made to her. There had been no rival within fifty miles.

Suddenly the three gentlemen who had fluttered around her own flame had been drawn away by a much brighter beacon. She recognized she could not hope to compete with Lady Grasset's weapons, could not outshine the woman with experience and worldliness and royal connections. She could only wait patiently and hope the gentlemen came to their senses and realized her own intrinsic value. It was a very frustrating situation, for she knew that intrinsic value was a dull and uninteresting counterweight to the superficial but sparkling attraction of accomplishment. She might sit by her hearth, filled with dignity, quiet wisdom and good will, but no one was going to know about all these qualities unless he made an effort to search them out. Nor would she entice with her beauty; she looked at herself carefully, after Lady Grasset's coup, and saw an appealing, clear-skinned, bright-eyed, brown-haired, twenty-seven-year-old woman—pretty, certainly, but not astonishingly so. She was, it was true, slender, while her rival was fat; but the flesh that had grown thick around Evelyn de Brey had not, apparently, smothered the woman's fascination.

Chastity did not have to ponder all these observations in a vacuum, exiled from society. Under the aegis of Lady Trentower she continued to go out and receive visitors, such as were still in London during this preseason period. Had she been more optimistic, in fact, she might have spared herself reflections upon lost suitors, for two of them visited her the day following their abduction.

The first was Mr. Brockton, who appeared early in the afternoon, glowing with goodwill and high spirits, quite as though nothing had happened.

His greeting from Lady Trentower was glacial. "Well, sir," she said accusingly.

Chastity was more civil, but scarcely more welcoming. "How do you do, Mr. Brockton," she said quietly, her expression blank.

Since Lady Trentower's greeting was unanswerable, he replied to Chastity. "Very well, indeed," he said enthusiastically. "It has been many months since I have been in London, and I must say I had forgotten how very lively the place can be. Of course, during my past trips I have not had the honor of being received by three of this city's most charming women." He bowed to Lady Trentower, who sat as erect as a sergeant major, and stared icily back at him.

"Three, sir?" she said. "Who might the third be?"

"Why, your own sister, ma'am," said the guileless Mr. Brockton with a good-natured smile. "I feel that very few men can be as lucky as I, for I had been in this immense city only a few hours, and during a visit to my charming neighbor," he gave Chastity what, for him, was an arch look, "I happened to meet not only yourself—delightful encounter!—but also your most attractive sister." He beamed at the two women. "Now, I ask you, are there many men as fortunate as I?"

Neither woman appeared pleased by Mr. Brockton's good luck. Lady Trentower, unbending, said, "If you are referring to Lady Grasset, sir, as I told you she is not really my sister, though she persists in spreading the fiction that she is."

"But," said Mr. Brockton, surprised, "did she not marry your brother?"

"Yes."

"Well, then," he said, "she is indeed your sister, for when one takes the sacred vows of marriage, one always acquires more than just a spouse—those who are truly blessed acquire a whole family." He paused significantly and smiled tenderly at Chastity, who remained impassive. "Your brother, ma'am," he said to Lady Trentower, "not only gained himself a most delightful wife, he also made you the gift of a charming sister."

Lady Trentower chose not to reply, but rather to regard Mr. Brockton as though he had begun to rave. Chastity filled the gap left by her aunt's ominous silence. "Did you have a pleasant afternoon, then, sir?" she asked politely, but without warmth.

"Pleasant! How weak the word is, my dear Miss Dalrymple. Let us say instead that I found an enchanting interlude in this large and bustling city." He smiled at the two women. "Of course, how could it be anything else since it began right here in the company of two of the most delectable women in London." He was quite carried away by his own gallantry. The two women continued to regard him with marked impartiality. "Then I was granted the honor of acting as escort to yet another delightful creature—all in the space of a few hours." He paused and solemnly turned to Chastity. "I realize, Miss Dalrymple, that I have you to thank for gaining me entry into these most elevated and hospitable circles. Do not think I am not grateful."

Chastity found it detestable to be thanked for having accomplished something she would just as soon had never come to pass. Although she did not regard Mr. Brockton as a possible spouse, she still was incensed at his defection. He might have understood that since his standing was so low he should have tried all the harder to gain her favor. She could not forgive him, among other things, for behaving with the confidence of someone whose position was secure. She retained, however, her polite impassivity as she said, "I am delighted to have been of service to you, sir."

Lady Trentower's indignation was not capable of subduing her curiosity, and she asked in a stentorian voice, "Where did you go, sir?"

"Why, I daresay we stopped in at every worthwhile drawing room in London," said Mr. Brockton. "Lady Grasset, as, of course, you know, only deals with... *la crème de la crème.*"

"Perhaps," said Lady Trentower coldly, "you would care to be more specific."

"Well, there was Lady Holland—what a noble woman—and Lady Bandrum; there was Lady Carruthers, the very essence of aristocracy, and Lady Dassington. Can you imagine being received by four such unparalleled women?"

"I have no need to imagine the situation, sir. I have lived it. Several times. All those women are well known to me."

"It does not surprise me that you would be among their number."

"What is surprising is that they all received Lady Grasset," said Lady Trentower in an unguarded moment of frankness.

At first Mr. Brockton did not recognize the ill-will that informed the remark. Instead he said enthusiastically, "But surely you recognize, ma'am, that quality will find quality." Then, dimly sensing there might be some animosity, he said placatingly, "And how Lady Grasset praised you, ma'am. I am sure your ears must have been burning all the afternoon."

"What did she say about me?" asked Lady Trentower sternly.

"Why, that you were her dear husband's very accomplished and wise sister, and that he had nothing but fond thoughts for you, and that she had heard so much about you while she was in Saint Petersburg that you were the first person she wished to see when she returned to London. She said, so sincerely you would blush, ma'am, she was not disappointed. All the good reports, even though they were colored by a brother's affection, were not in the least exaggerated. You have lived up to her expectations." Mr. Brockton smiled triumphantly as he delivered this encomium.

Lady Trentower's face was contorted with distaste. "You will forgive me, sir," she said chillingly, "if I do not lose myself in transports of joy at learning I have lived up to the expectations of a woman who...well, let us say simply that I do not consider Lady Grasset capable of establishing a criteria worth striving toward."

Though Mr. Brockton was not delicate in judging human relations, he did perceive finally that an endorsement of Lady Grasset would accomplish nothing for him in this particular drawing room. He was mired so deeply in his public enthusiasm for the woman, however, that he could not withdraw abruptly without appearing fickle. "Ah, well," he said judiciously, "you know, ma'am, that it was your brother who inspired her great regard. It was not *she* who created the high standards she expected to find in you..."

"My brother and I," said Lady Trentower relentlessly, "did not so much as exchange a note during his last years, and before he went to Russia we spoke only when we happened to find ourselves face to face at some public gathering. There was no animosity between us; but there was no nonsense about our mutual excellence. It would astonish me if during his time in Russia William suddenly began to endow me with qualities. If he did such a thing—and I cannot for a moment believe it—they would have to be mythical. No, sir.

Lady Grasset, I believe, has been overwhelmed by fancy. That is the kindest interpretation I can put on her most bizarre remarks."

Mr. Brockton appeared crushed. Chastity could see the magnificent edifice of his immediate social life, of which Lady Trentower's drawing room was no doubt the cornerstone, crumble before his dismayed eyes. Even though he had, she felt, behaved badly the day before, she took pity on him, and saved him the humiliation of responding to Lady Trentower by asking, "Did Mr. Techett and Count Orlanov also accompany you on your visits?"

"Yes," said Mr. Brockton, still dazed by the awful realization that something had gone wrong. "Indeed they did. Very fine gentlemen. Splendid fellows." He tried to speak robustly, but his heart was not in it.

"It sounds," said Lady Trentower, "like a regular little army. No doubt it shall grow in size as the length of her stay increases."

"Ha, ha," laughed Mr. Brockton. Though he had finally realized how the land lay, he was not up to commenting beyond this show of forlorn mirth. He looked around a little sadly, and said to Chastity, "I anticipate seeing a great deal of you while I am in London, Miss Dalrymple. I do hope you will not be too busy to receive an old and very respectful neighbor."

"Not at all, sir," said Chastity coldly. She was somewhat mollified by his confusion, for it was, in a sense, a form of contrition. But she was not yet ready to forgive; and certainly his chances of winning her hand were even more remote than they had been at Grangeford. After a few more remarks of a general and polite nature, Mr. Brockton took his leave.

As soon as the door was shut, Lady Trentower said, "Well, the man has been brought to his senses, I believe. For a few moments he sounded like a lunatic." She looked appraisingly at Chastity. "You could do worse. I think he will come round."

With that remark she snapped the delicate alliance that had been spun between herself and her niece. Chastity was appalled that her aunt would assume she could ever accept such a humdrum suitor. She turned the chill she had reserved for Mr. Brockton toward Lady Trentower. "Whether he comes round or no is of no concern to me."

"Nonsense," said Lady Trentower, annoyed. "Don't be coy with me, my girl. Of course you care. You are not in a position to be all that choosy."

Chastity rose with dignity. "I must write some letters," she said, and left without looking back.

Barely half an hour later she was summoned again to the drawing room with the announcement that Mr. Techett was paying a call. She received this news with a tremor of apprehension, and hastily checked herself in the long mirror of her sitting room. She was looking, she decided gratefully, very well—color good, and eyes bright and clear. She pinched her cheeks and pressed and puckered her lips, and descended again to the drawing room.

Charles Techett was speaking to Lady Trentower as she entered, "... and then we left Lady Holland's and went to Lady Carruther's (who inquired most closely about you, ma'am, and asked that I convey her regards if I should see you before she had that pleasure) then..." He stopped when he saw Chastity, and rose. His face, she noticed, was as unclouded with remorse as Mr. Brockton's. He looked remarkably at ease.

"Charles is just giving an account of his afternoon yesterday," said Lady Trentower affably. She smiled in a feline manner with her lips; her eyes sent out signals of repressed rancor. "It appears our guests left here for a quite lively round of visiting."

Charles's smile was slow and faintly ironical. "I can assure you, ma'am, that my stop here was the high point of my day."

"That is good to know," said Lady Trentower drily. "How was Lady Grasset received elsewhere?"

"Very well. How would you expect your sister-in-law to be received, if not with flourishes of delight and honor?" His voice was teasing.

Lady Trentower was not amused. "Surely there was condescension on the part of those she visited," she stated, rather than asked.

"None that I could discern," said Charles blandly.

"I suppose," said Lady Trentower, frowning thoughtfully, "that they feel they owe it to me to be kind to the woman."

"Very possibly," said Charles, a glint of amusement in his eye, "although my impression is that most of the people Lady Grasset meets succumb to her charms, and end up liking her for herself."

"Her charms? Pray, what might they be?" asked Lady Trentower challengingly.

"She is fresh and vivacious and amusing. She has a lively interest in her surroundings that is appealing, I think. She is direct and open in her enthusiasms, and pursues her goal—which is to ingratiate herself with society—without dissimulation. And, of course, she is close to the Grand Duchess and, one assumes, the Tsar."

"She is fat," said Lady Trentower.

Charles retained an amused front. "Surely you do not judge character by such superficial standards?"

"I have always thought that physical appearance is a perfect indication of one's personal worth," said Lady Trentower. "I have never subscribed to the foolish and sentimental fallacy that the one has no bearing on the other."

"It is true," said Charles, "that Lady Grasset is larger than when she left, but you must admit that she has retained many fine features. The eyes are as brilliant as ever, and the complexion is astonishing in its glowing translucence. Her hands and feet are small and delicate, and she moves very gracefully."

Lady Trentower would have made some objection, but Chastity was becoming depressed by Charles's recitation of Lady Grasset's qualities, and everything her aunt said seemed calculated to make him extend the catalog. In order to staunch the flow of praise she interrupted by asking, "Is Lady Grasset going to remain in England?"

Charles turned to her with a subtle but gratifying change of expression; his glance lost its teasing overtones. "I do not know. I wonder whether even Lady Grasset knows, at this point. It would seem the logical thing for her to do. But, on the other hand, she has lived for ten years in Russia, and must have many ties there it would be painful to break."

"Yes," said Lady Trentower. "One wonders how long she will continue to trail one of those 'ties' after her if she decides to stay." She looked from Charles to Chastity and back again with a disapproving air. "I am speaking, of course, of that mute count who is always at her side."

"Count Orlanov is not mute," said Chastity involuntarily.

"He might as well be for all he contributes to conversation."

"He can be... very loquacious if he chooses," Chastity began to blush.

Charles had compressed his lips when the count was mentioned. He said coldly, "Count Orlanov is merely an escort for Lady Grasset."

"Surely you don't believe that," said Lady Trentower derisively. "All London knows the man is her lover."

"All London has been mistaken in other similar circumstances."

"But not in this one, I think," said Lady Trentower. "I shall be very surprised if you persist in maintaining that Lady Grasset's relationship to that man is innocent."

"Because there is no evidence to the contrary, that is precisely what I believe." Charles had lost his playfulness. His face was a little flushed and his black eyes glinted. Chastity watched him with growing distress, for he was so obviously jealous.

"Evidence! Why the man is like her shadow! I have never seen her without him. What more evidence do you need?" Lady Trentower was disdainful. She looked around the room as though it were filled with corroborating witnesses.

"I would hardly call the public presence of an

escort an indication of dalliance. Lady Grasset is a woman of some importance in the retinue of the Grand Duchess. It is only natural that she should be accompanied by an aide."

"I do not call it natural," said Lady Trentower.

"We are not familiar with the customs of the Russian court," said Charles with suppressed annoyance. "I assume it is usual to send women of rank into society with a male escort. There is nothing sinister in the arrangement."

It was Lady Trentower's turn to express ironic amusement. "My dear Charles, we are not in Russia. And even if we were, I should be astonished to discover that the distance of a few thousand miles could wreak such changes on human nature as to modify the significance of a man's perpetual attendance upon a lone woman. You may mark my words, even though it is true that I am ignorant of the customs of that barbaric court—that Lady Grasset is currently adorned with a lover."

Charles smiled thinly, noticeably put out. After hesitating he said, "I must bow, I suppose, to your superior intuition. It is one of the most potent weapons of your sex. But in my own very foolish male way, I cannot help but harbor the suspicion you might be mistaken."

"Perhaps," said Lady Trentower with arched brows, "it is because you have discovered a rekindling of your own former interest that you so tenaciously insist upon the matter." The remark was uncommonly straightforward, even for her, and it made Chastity's eyes widen with surprise. Charles, however, regained his cool amused mask, and merely shook his head slightly.

"Though I find Lady Grasset extremely agreeable, as, I trust, she does me, I can assure you that our mutual pleasure in each other is only social." His tone was even, almost bored, and he continued smiling as though at some private joke.

"I am glad to hear it, my dear Charles," said Lady Trentower, looking at him as though she did not believe a word of what he had said, "for I do not think it would be wise for you to marry the woman."

"How you do go on," said Charles with a laugh. "I hope this piece of gossip is not circulating. I fear it would harm Lady Grasset's reputation to be linked with one as stodgy and dull as I."

Chastity watched him closely, but was unable to ascertain whether he was sincere in his protestation. After exposing the brief flash of annoyance, he had assumed again that glossy and impenetrable shield of amused detachment; it was impossible to tell what he was really thinking or if, by some happenstance, he actually meant what he was saying. Chastity was growing more and more uncomfortable as her aunt continued to goad Charles into positions where he had little choice but to defend Lady Grasset. He was being forced to champion her even if he had not wanted to. This circumstance made her more hostile than usual toward the old woman.

She, however, like Charles Techett, showed nothing, but sat with a slight smile on her lips, her hands languidly folded in her lap. She gazed at Charles and her aunt alike with indifference, making sure her glance displayed not one scintilla of her true feelings.

Charles stood. "I fear I must be on my way," he said pleasantly. He bowed to both women, and, after a few automatic and cursory protestations from Lady Trentower that he remain a while longer, he took his leave. Chastity waited for some special sign, some indication of particular attention from him. There was none. She watched him go with a black, hollow emptiness, though her smile never faltered.

"Well," said Lady Trentower, nodding her head, "we shall soon be hearing more about this situation."

Chastity had to quell her impulse to snap at the woman. After a brief pause she said, "Mr. Techett did not seem to me to be particularly smitten by Lady Grasset."

"Ha!" said Lady Trentower. "Of course not. But perhaps you noticed how he bridled at the mention of the woman's lover. That was not an indifferent reaction. Mark my words, we shall have a scandal soon." She nodded her head several times with satisfaction. "It's just as well his initial attention to you never grew into anything more noticeable, for you would be swept into the gossip that will inevitably surround that pair. You would be regarded as an object of pity—never a vantage point from which to look for a husband."

At that moment Chastity was already regarding herself as an object of pity because of Charles Techett's indifferent departure; furthermore she held her aunt's indelicate and persistent prying responsible for having forced him to signal more concern for Lady Grasset than he would have if the subject had not been so relentlessly pursued. She could not, under the combined strain of self-pity and hostility, maintain her facade of cool indifference. She turned on her aunt with sudden and surprising vehemence. "What Mr. Techett does, and who he does it with, is of absolutely no concern to me. I am not interested in this sort of scandal-mongering that seems to occupy such a large part of the lives of you who live in London. Now I must finish my letters."

For the second time that day she strode from the room with a set face and angry eyes. Lady Trentower watched her go with a cocked eyebrow and a small smile.

Chapter Six

It was three days before Lady Grasset called again, and this hiatus caused apprehension in the breasts of both Lady Trentower and Chastity. Lady Trentower, though professing to despise her sister-in-law, was forced nevertheless to acknowledge that the relationship had its advantages: Lady Grasset's connection to the Grand Duchess Catherine had rubbed off on her, Lady Trentower, so that many of her acquaintances had begun to hint they would be most grateful if she could put in a word with her relation in order that they might be presented. Lady Trentower, of course, deplored this sort of machination, and resolutely turned her nose up whenever she was thus approached. She did, however, relish the power that snubbing others and saying "no" to them invested in her, and did not wish to lose it because of an open and complete break with Lady Grasset. She fretted that perhaps she had been a little too ungracious with the woman, and had thus discouraged her from calling again. She wondered whether she should drop a note—nothing friendly; merely a cold inquiry as to the state of her health.

Chastity's apprehension was twofold. First, she wished to inspect Lady Grasset again, to evaluate her anew, now she had admitted rivalry. This was a desire akin to the impulse that makes one prod a wound to ascertain whether it is still painful. Second, she wished to see Count Orlanov, and it was impossible to find that gentleman beyond the shadow of Lady Grasset. She wanted to test her own feelings for him, as well as to learn whether his ardor had increased or cooled after the avowals he had whispered into her ear while leaning so close that she could still imagine the sweetness of his breath.

Neither aunt nor niece spoke of her uneasiness at the prolonged absence of Lady Grasset, but both paid inordinate attention to the detailed journalistic accounts of the Grand Duchess's movements in and around the capital, and both made frequent trips to windows to check inhabitants of carriages as they clattered through the streets below.

It was after just such a trip that Lady Trentower, peering through a discreetly parted curtain, announced with mingled triumph and outrage, "Imagine who has come to see me!" Disdainfully she dropped the curtain and assumed a nonchalant pose on one of her little gilt chairs. Chastity did not bother to respond, for she knew immediately who had arrived, and she set about making herself equally unconcerned.

The door burst open and Lady Grasset rushed in. "You see, dear sister," she said gaily, "how I am without formality with you. Your man asked how I should be announced and I replied 'Not at all,' for I am one of the family, *n'est-ce pas?*" Though she was still mammoth, she appeared to Chastity to be quite pretty. Against the black silk of her dress her skin did indeed glow, just as Charles Techett had proclaimed so effusively, and her eyes sparkled beneath their long lashes. Her lips were parted in breathless anticipation of some pleasant event, and she floated along the floor light as a balloon. "I almost feared to come, for I know I have been remiss in staying away such a long while without sending word. You will, I hope, forgive me when I tell you I have had to spend hours and hours in Parliament."

"Parliament?" said Lady Trentower dubiously.

"I was sent by the Grand Duchess to see whether she would be at ease there—she trusts no one but me in these matters—so of course I was obliged to ascertain that there were adequate facilities for the comfort of a woman of the Grand Duchess's rank. This meant sitting through several debates in order to get the feeling of what my dear friend might be expected to experience."

"You have been visiting Parliament?" said Lady Trentower to make sure she had heard correctly. She looked disapproving.

"I hope," said Chastity, "you found your visit worthwhile and devoid of tedium." Her smile was slight and polite.

Lady Grasset placed her hands on her bosom. "I wept!"

"Whatever for?" said Lady Trentower.

"The majesty! The superb machinery of a free nation grinding out justice and laws! But you, of course, surely know better than I of what I speak."

"I have never been," said Lady Trentower. "Will you take tea?"

Count Orlanov had, as was his wont, followed Lady Grasset at a distance and, after bowing silently to the two women, had stood rigidly by one of the gilt chairs waiting for an invitation to be seated. He was, again, wearing the white and gold uniform and carrying the white casque with its jet of crimson feathers. His handsome, regular features were composed, his blue eyes stared straight ahead. Light glinted almost as effectively from the curls on his head and the thick moustache as from the gold braid of his uniform.

"Won't you be seated, sir," said Chastity with a pleasant but impersonal expression.

With military precision he folded himself onto the chair, placed his casque on the floor, and sat upright at attention.

Lady Grasset addressed Lady Trentower exclusively, who replied with a mélange of wariness and distaste, though she was a mite more circumspect now that her sister-in-law had become someone to reckon with in society. Chastity was on the periphery of their conversation, and was able to slip in and out of it as inconspicuously as a fly. To Count Orlanov she said quietly, "Did you also visit Parliament, sir?"

With his fierce blue eyes full on her he replied, "Yes, ma'am, I did. It was an extraordinary experience, one that cannot be duplicated in my homeland. This exposure to English politics plus my finding someone as delightful as you inhabiting the country has made me wonder whether to settle here permanently."

Reflecting swiftly, Chastity surmised she had been pronounced comparable to Parliament; she found the comparison not particularly flattering. But a glance at Count Orlanov, leaning toward her, disposed of her cavil. "How kind, sir," she murmured, eyes downcast. "So you might stay in England? Will you remain in London if that is your decision?"

"I will go wherever my heart is led. You can answer your own question, for the reins are in your delicate hands." He spoke so solemnly, and his stare was so piercing, that Chastity could not discount his words with badinage. She was so tense she held her breath. Expelling a quiet, determined sigh, she looked directly into his eyes.

"Sir, you have made me the recipient of frequent compliments of an exaggerated kind. You seem to assume that you can discuss with me your most intimate concerns, without having established whether or no your intentions are honorable. I am not familiar with the customs of your country, but I can tell you, sir, that such behavior violates the usages of mine."

Undeterred, Count Orlanov said, "You mean that I should declare my wish to marry you before stating that I find you desirable."

That was precisely what Chastity meant, but she would have preferred that it be stated less baldly. She looked at her hands an instant, then raised her eyes again to his. "These things take more time than you have allowed. We have scarcely seen each other. You have not spoken to my parent and established your intentions. I know nothing of you—nor you of me. We only know what we have been able to perceive during a few brief meetings."

"To whom shall I speak? To your aunt?" he asked abruptly.

The idea of Count Orlanov asking permission of Lady Trentower to pursue her hand in marriage made Chastity quake. "No, sir. Ordinarily a gentleman who wishes to declare himself a suitor speaks to the lady's father. My father, of course is not in London...."

"I will go to him."

"He is in Kent, sir, a good two days' journey from here."

"What is two days to me, with such a prize at the end of them?"

"Can you leave London at your own whim, sir?" asked Chastity.

"I shall have to make arrangements." There was a slight falter in his voice. "But I shall be able to leave within a week or so."

"Are your emotions genuinely at liberty, sir? Do you not have commitments...elsewhere?"

Count Orlanov paused the briefest instant. "My emotions are in your power."

"I confess I do not understand your ardor," said Chastity with an involuntary shake of her head.

"What is there to understand? I saw you, I wanted you," he said, causing Chastity to look at him with startled eyes. He leaned closer. "What is troubling you? Do you not like me? Do not tell me no, for I would not believe you. I am not speaking from conceit, but from instinct. I know that there is a bond between us."

"But I am so unlike...the women you know. The other women who are in your world." She could not prevent a cautious glance toward Lady Grasset, who was animatedly chattering away to Lady Trentower.

"That is true," said Count Orlanov, with increased fervor, "you are unlike anyone I have ever met."

Chastity sat back to gain perspective. She was as sensitive to the man's appearance, to his odor of leather and cologne, his taut musculature that could be discerned under the fine white fabric—she was as sensitive to all these aspects as to what he was saying. What he was saying indubitably was that he wished to marry her. This was a suitor, certainly, who could not be faulted for a lack of dash. If anything, he had too much. She thought apprehensively that if she were the tiniest bit more encouraging he would toss her over his shoulder and carry her to Saint Petersburg. She did not enjoy this brief fantasy; rather, it made her doubt his stability and even his sincerity, for perhaps there was something too theatrical in his protestations, something not quite genuine. For all his surface passion he might well be harboring deceit. How could she know, for she had no key to his character. He was an exotic, and though she would have protested if she had been accused of it, she shared her countrymen's distrust of foreigners.

Yet there was no question of terminating Count Orlanov's advances. If she even wavered in that direction, one whiff of the man, one glance at his magnificent torso, one fleeting remembrance of the feel of his arm about her waist as they danced, would have been enough to shatter her resolve. When she was with him she found him, quite simply, fascinating in the strictest sense of the word: she was spellbound. Even this conversation they were holding, whispering under the noses of her two aunts, had an element of enchantment and make-believe. How bizarre to be discussing such passionate topics while seated on two of the most conventional gilt chairs in one of the most conventional drawing rooms in London, sipping tea, guarding expressions that would have indicated to any observer they were obviously chatting about nothing more startling than, say, the season's first daffodil in Hyde Park.

Carefully Chastity placed her cup on the small table in front of them. "And you," she replied with bewildered conviction, "are unlike anyone *I* have ever met."

Across the room Lady Grasset broke into cheerful laughter. Chastity was afraid she had been overheard, but a quick glance revealed that the rollicking response was to something said by a dour and unbending Lady Trentower.

Cautiously Chastity waited to be sure both her aunts were engaged with each other before saying, even more quietly than before, "Have you ... have you no present attachment, sir?"

"To you."

"I mean, is there no one to whom you owe allegiance?"

Count Orlanov did not blink, but he remained silent an instant too long. "Everyone has attachments of some sort."

"I do not."

"You are a woman. I meant every man."

Ridiculously the image of Joseph Brockton flashed through Chastity's mind. She was certain no attachments lurked in that quarter. The thought departed as rapidly as it had come, and she said, "That may be. I do not know. But what is of importance to the present is whether you are currently maintaining ... affection for someone." Again she could not restrain a glance to Lady Grasset.

"There is no affection I have to hide."

With a deep sigh, Chastity said, "Sir, are you Lady Grasset's lover?"

Count Orlanov showed neither surprise nor displeasure; he was quiet for a few seconds. Then, "You will understand that I am not at liberty to discuss a matter which would reflect on a lady's honor. I have not the right to answer your question."

Ordinarily Chastity subscribed to the convention that prompted his answer; of course no gentleman should ever jeopardize a lady's reputation. But this situation did seem to her to be somewhat beyond the pale of such covenants, even as this peculiar wooing departed so radically from the usual methods. His evasion made it quite clear that he was involved with Lady Grasset. What she wished to determine was the extent of his commitment, but she assumed that such a revelation was inimical to his code, and did not press the matter.

"You understand, then, sir, that under the circumstances I cannot entertain any further discussion of an intimate nature with you." She spoke more as a diplomat delivers a formal ultimatum to be disputed, than from conviction.

Count Orlanov was thoughtful. "Life is very complex, and very surprising. There are events which no one could guess, and which would be ridiculed as lacking verisimilitude if presented on the stage in even the most farfetched melodramas. I have been swept into one of those events, Miss Dalrymple. Believe me, I am honorable, as are all the other participants. Believe me, that my involvement in no way diminishes the feelings I have for you."

Chastity mulled that over. Across the room Lady Grasset laughed again, and Chastity gave her another surreptitious glance. Her eyes returned to Count Orlanov, who sat staring at her solemnly. She had never seen the man smile, and certainly had never heard him laugh. Was he as intense with Lady Grasset as with her? And just what, she wondered further, did this intensity signify? At the moment he was obviously waiting for her to comment on his extraordinary pronouncement; he was watching her the way a sailor scans the horizon for signs of a storm. "Life *is* surprising, sir," she said with a nervous and subdued laugh. "Indeed, I could not have imagined this conversation. Particularly upon such short acquaintance. I cannot offer any opinion upon your statement, obviously. I presume you will clarify the matter shortly."

Count Orlanov shrugged. "Clarification is not within my power. However, I have no doubt that there will be enlightenment soon." Chastity could make no answer to this cryptic remark, but the count did not expect one, for he continued, "I shall go to your father within a week to ask for your hand in marriage."

"I think that, under the circumstances, that would be premature..." Chastity said, surprised.

Lady Grasset laughed again, more loudly and insistent. "Oh, you have such a wicked tongue," she said, her hand to her chest, as she gazed fondly at Lady Trentower. "I am grateful that as your sister I can assume I am excluded from its venom." She glanced playfully at Chastity. "Don't you find your aunt's sharpness a challenge?" she asked lightly. "I envy your greater exposure to it, for no doubt you can cope with it much better than I."

Lady Trentower sat as straight on her chair as Count Orlanov on his, showing by her general mien that she recognized the blatant flattery, and refused to be taken in by it. Chastity smiled noncommittally.

"But how I've neglected you, my dear niece," said Lady Grasset, unperturbed by this tepid behavior. "I have been so eager to have a little chat with you ever since I met your beau."

"My beau?" said Chastity.

Lady Grasset smiled teasingly and wagged a pudgy finger. "She doesn't know who I'm talking about," she said playfully. "A certain Mr. J.B. would be desolate to hear that, were I naughty enough to tell him. But I shall not, for I could not bear to bring pain to such a delightful, such a spirited gentleman."

"Are you talking about Mr. Brockton?" Lady Trentower asked briskly.

"That is his name," said Lady Grasset.

"Mr. Brockton," said Chastity quietly, "is our neighbor in Kent. That is all."

"But soon, if he has his way, he will be much more than a neighbor," said Lady Grasset. Her smile was open and friendly.

"I fear you have been misinformed," said Chastity, blushing. "Mr. Brockton is an excellent gentleman, and no doubt honorable, but he is, and shall remain, merely a neighbor."

"You will break his heart," said Lady Grasset with mock sadness. It was evident that she did not believe Chastity's denial.

"Actually," said Lady Trentower, "I was much

impressed by the gentleman myself, and confess that I am at a loss as to my niece's reluctance to encourage the man in his attentions."

Under any circumstances Chastity would have found this conversation obnoxious, but held under the nose of Count Orlanov it was intolerable. She was furious that her younger aunt agreed with the older that Joseph Brockton was a suitable match for her. Further denial, she knew, would only prolong the discussion, so she smiled coldly and said nothing. She could not, however, banish the blush that flooded her face and neck.

"I have always believed," said Lady Grasset lightheartedly, "that actions speak louder than words. A look at my dear niece's color indicates to me that she is not indifferent to her worthy neighbor."

Chastity rose abruptly. "Please excuse me," she said with stony-faced composure, "I am unwell."

Immediately Count Orlanov stood. Chastity scanned his face, looking for some private message; she saw, however, only rigid good manners. She walked rapidly from the gathering before either Lady Grasset or Lady Trentower had time to comment.

Once in her rooms she felt more foolish and awkward than at any time since her adolescence. During those years, in fact, she had more composure than to flee a drawing room so precipitately. She could not, however, have countenanced the situation another moment: Not only was she being foisted off on the dreary Mr. Brockton, but the only rival she ever had was party to the transaction. As soon as she had become a little more calm she admitted she was escaping Count Orlanov's imperturbable stare and mystifying advances as well as Lady Grasset's elephantine teasing. The man confused her, and she was angry at herself for not having the courage to tell him to cease his foolishness and go about his business. Always in the past she had controlled the people and events that threatened her calm; if by no other means she would dismiss or ignore them. She had not the will to do either this time, for while one part of her recognized that the count's bizarre behavior was hardly proper, another part of her was so drawn to the man—to his handsomeness and mystery—that she could not bear to give him up so long as he continued to pursue her. She was certain that if he were to stop his pursuit she would not only make no effort to revive his interest, she would actually be relieved. Perhaps, she thought, it was only her vanity, and not her heart, that was meshed into the courtship. This was not an attractive state of affairs, in her judgment, but she seemed incapable of modifying her feelings.

She sulked in her rooms, and even refused to descend to dinner. When Lady Trentower sent an inquiry as to whether she wished to go to the opera as planned, she excused herself with a curt message that she was retiring early.

Nor did she descend to breakfast the next day, but prolonged her solitude until she became so bored that even the prospect of conversation with her aunt was less onerous than remaining for another moment by herself. She went down to the morning room where Lady Trentower sat surrounded by the day's newspapers.

"Imagine," Lady Trentower said without any further greeting, "the woman actually did go to

Parliament—dragging along her whole retinue by the sound of it, and at the end of the day she was heard to comment," here she raised her voice to a high and unpleasant pitch, " 'Your Parliament is a wonderful institution. If I were an Englishman, I would never leave it.' What nonsense! If she were an Englishman she would not talk such foolishness in the hearing of people who would scribble it down and publish it for all the world to read." She threw down the journal she had been reading, and picked up another.

"Are they quoting Lady Grasset?" asked Chastity.

"No, of course not, you silly child. They are quoting the Grand Duchess Catherine." She made a disapproving click with her tongue, before adding, "Really this is too shameful. Just look at the columns they have devoted to the woman." She began to read avidly, her eyes darting through the newsprint at a great clip. She arrived at the end of the account with an exasperated sigh, and immediately reached for another paper. She paused and looked closely at Chastity. "Are you feeling better?" she asked without any concern in her voice.

"Yes, thank you."

"Splendid," said Lady Trentower drily. "Then you will be able to attend the little 'at-home' given by the Grand Duchess tomorrow. If you wish. I accepted for you, but there is no need to be bound by that."

"Who issued the invitation?" asked Chastity.

"Who do you think? My sister-in-law, of course." The tartness in Lady Trentower's voice now seemed almost to derive from habit rather than conviction. She plunged into another account of the Grand Duchess's sortie.

"It is curious," said Chastity, "that Lady Grasset did not accompany her patroness to Parliament."

"She met her there. Apparently shortly after she left here. It is all recorded—appalling, the trivia these papers see fit to print." She continued reading as she spoke.

Chastity had no inclination to read any of the journals in the large pile around her aunt's feet. The thought of Lady Grasset made her feel sour. "The at-home will be held at the Pulteney Hotel?" she asked, injecting a false idleness into her voice.

"Where else? She has no other home on these shores." Lady Trentower briefly looked up. "You will go then?" There was a glint of sardonic amusement in her eyes.

"I don't know," said Chastity stiffly.

"It will be quite an occasion, from what my sister-in-law tells me. All London will be there—not that I would consider that an inducement, of course. You, however, should be seen at affairs of this sort."

"Why?" asked Chastity reflexively, and immediately regretted it, for she anticipated the answer.

"Because," said Lady Trentower, lowering her paper, "you are hunting a husband, and it is at such gatherings as the one tomorrow where husbands are to be found." She returned to her paper.

Chastity set her mouth and narrowed her eyes.

Lady Trentower, her attention still fixed on the newspaper, added, "Your Mr. Brockton will be there. Or at least he has been invited." She was silent an instant. "Of course, Charles Techett will be there. *She* has seen to that, I'm sure." She turned the pages of the paper rapidly, scanning each. "Who knows? It might be that some gentleman you have not yet seen—or, more to the point, who has not yet seen you—will appear and find you fetching enough to pursue your hand. Stranger things have happened." She put the paper down and looked blandly at her niece.

Chastity returned the look with open dislike, but did not protest.

Chapter Seven

Gusts of wind and rain against her window panes woke Chastity the following day. The sky was gray and gloomy, more like winter than spring, and the house was cold. Lady Trentower was a great respector of seasons, and, short of a blizzard, had no intention of violating the springtime with fires in the grates. She did pay obeisance to the reality of the weather with a shawl thrown around her bony shoulders.

"A dreadful day for a reception," she said to Chastity by way of greeting. "I should not be surprised if half London stayed home." She was pleased at this possibility; at the same time she made it clear that she was not a member of that fainthearted half. "I have called for the coach at two-thirty. The invitation is for two."

Chastity nodded. She went to the sideboard where the array of breakfast dishes gleamed under the glow of candles the gloomy day made necessary. She had little appetite, however, and took a small biscuit and tea.

"You'll need more than that," said Lady Trentower, "to get you through the day. It's all very well to appear finicky and delicate in public but here you're with your old aunt, and have no reason for airs. Take some fish." There were the remains of a substantial breakfast on her own plate.

"I am not hungry," said Chastity crossly.

"A mistake," said Lady Trentower. "A big breakfast, I have always held, is the foundation of true beauty." She unconsciously caressed her own gray ringlets that peeked from under her lace morning cap. "*I* have breakfasted copiously every day of my life."

Chastity nibbled morosely on her biscuit.

"It is essential," continued Lady Trentower didactically, "that you look as well as possible now, and since you can no longer boast the bloom of youth, you must exhibit vivacity. A display of energy can mask any number of drawbacks; even the unfortunate fact that you have progressed far beyond the age of twenty—which is the prime age for marriage for a woman, in my estimation—can be overlooked, temporarily, at least, if you are sufficiently animated." She lowered her voice confidentially. "A biscuit, my dear, is not sufficient nourishment to inspire that activity and brightness you must command in order to disguise your twenty-seven years. Do take some fish."

Chastity placed her half-eaten biscuit on the plate and said, "I am not hungry. If I were I would eat. Pray let us discuss the matter no further."

Lady Trentower stiffened and pursed her lips. "You should have a care, my dear, to guard against a too waspish disposition. No man wants to wed a shrew." She paused thoughtfully. "Unless, of course, her fortune is enormous. Your dowry, however substantial, will not efface a certain abrasiveness that surfaces from time to time when you are unwary. I am sure," she added sweetly, "that it was not your intention to snap at me just now, but that is the unfortunate impression I received."

Chastity breathed deeply several times, then rose from the table. "I shall be ready at two-thirty," she said, and left the dining room, her biscuit and tea unfinished. Lady Trentower raised her brows, shook her head and clicked her tongue. Then she returned to the sideboard and helped herself to some nuts.

At exactly two-thirty Chastity went to the drawing room, where she found Lady Trentower and Charles Techett waiting for her.

"Look who has come to fetch us," said Lady Trentower gaily. She was wearing a deep blue silk dress and her face was artfully painted to just this side of garishness. She was, Chastity had to admit, quite handsome. Charles was affable and admiring as he bowed his greeting.

"I hope I have not kept you waiting," said Chastity.

"I would have waited for hours, if necessary, for the appearance of such a delight."

"Not at all," said Lady Trentower, cutting through Charles's gallantry. "You are very punctual."

Chastity was already wearing a light beige woolen cloak over her white muslin dress, so Charles helped Lady Trentower into her dark blue cape.

"What a nasty day," said the old woman cheerfully. "I'm glad it is not I who is receiving today, for I fear my drawing room would be quite sparsely inhabited." She led the way to the foyer, buoyed with the anticipation of witnessing someone else's debacle.

She was, however, to be disappointed, for as the carriage approached the Pulteney Hotel, the press of other vehicles slowed them to a crawl. There was an even greater crowd attending the Grand Duchess's reception than had been to her ball. It put Lady Trentower out of humor. "Whatever can they be thinking of," she muttered, more or less to herself. "At this rate we shall spend the greater part of the afternoon in our carriage."

"I am quite well here," said Charles, "and could ask nothing better." He glanced quickly at Chastity, allowing his eyes to touch hers for a significant span. "I am fortunate to have found the best company—and the prettiest—in London."

Chastity smiled and dropped her gaze.

"How you do go on," said Lady Trentower fretfully as she looked out the window. "You can enjoy our company much better in a dry and warm drawing room. I hope they have the good sense to make fires. One never knows with foreigners."

"I daresay the Grand Duchess will see to our comfort adequately," said Charles. Again he looked at Chastity, this time with a conspiratorial smile.

At first Chastity was immensely heartened by these little attentions; she had been almost ready to believe that Lady Trentower was correct when she predicted that Charles soon would be accompanying Lady Grasset hither and yon. Immediately following her lift of gratification, however, came the recognition that she was dealing with a London gallant, and his glances, gestures and words might have no more significance than a pleasant and civilized greeting or farewell; it was possible he was simply being polite. The thought caused her to scan his face dubiously at the very moment he turned his eyes toward her. Instead of a soft, gently smiling, tender look he received a piercing, skeptical gaze of curiosity. Chastity dropped her eyes in confusion. The carriage reached the entrance of the hotel, and the door was opened by a footman bearing an umbrella.

"I thought we'd never arrive," said Lady Trentower.

Charles got out of the coach first and handed down Lady Trentower. He raised his hand and eyes to Chastity as she stepped to the pavement. "I hope," he said, "I will be honored with an explanation of that most disconcerting appraisal I have just received." Chastity blushed and quickly turned to disengage her skirt from the edge of the door. "For an instant," Charles said in a low voice, "I thought I was being scrutinized by a sphinx."

"Sphinx?" said Lady Trentower, who had been trying to hear what Charles was saying so softly, not because she wished to pry, but because she could not conceive that any conversation within her hearing was not directed solely to herself. "What's this about a sphinx?"

"I was merely alluding to an Egyptian statue," said Charles.

"I am aware of what the thing is," said Lady Trentower, annoyed, "but in what context are you discussing it?"

"Oh, just a little conversation about the merits of Egyptian and Russian art. A frivolous observation, not worth repeating." Charles presented both his arms to the aunt and niece and they moved under the canopy leading to the entrance of the hotel.

"Hmm," said Lady Trentower, still annoyed,

but already distracted by the abundance of elegant visitors sedately inching their way into the hotel. "My word," she said, "there's Lady Grunding. I could have sworn she was still in the country. Do you think she returned just for this?"

Neither Charles nor Chastity ventured an opinion. Chastity felt a slight squeeze as Charles pressed his arm against his side, catching her hand in a tender vise.

The foyer of the Pulteney Hotel remained as undistinguished as it had been for the ball: A few vases of hothouse flowers were the only acknowledgment of an event that was out of the ordinary. Most of the visitors streamed through it without noticing anyway, for all headed for the stairway leading to the second floor.

Grand Duchess Catherine had installed herself at the far end of the large room that had served for dancing at her ball. The room had been refurbished; the gilt of the reliefs on the ceiling gleamed and there were drapes of a regal crimson at the windows and behind a raised platform on which a large armchair, upholstered in the same hue, was placed. Because the weather was so dismal the candelabra were all put in service, and hundreds of flames extravagantly sparkling in the dim daylight created an atmosphere of opulence. Vases of roses and tulips were placed on pedestals along the creamy white walls, and a long crimson runner extended over the gleaming parquet floor from the entrance to the Grand Duchess.

As before, she was dressed in black, and was tiny, lively, and faintly malicious. If she was affected at all by the criticism directed at her lack of discretion concerning the Prince Regent she did not show it. Her intelligent eyes glinted with interest as they fell on each of her guests, and she accepted their compliments, good wishes, queries about how she was enjoying her stay, comments on the weather—accepted all with ironical good humor. There was not a suspicion of deference or swagger in her behavior. She was so at ease she might have been in Saint Petersburg.

"How do you do?" she greeted the cluster of Lady Trentower, Charles and Chastity. She held her hands out to them from her chair, but then withdrew them before they could be grasped. "How nice of you to brave your English weather for me. But then I suppose you are used to it. I am not. I do not like it."

Lady Trentower turned rigid with disapproval. "Our climate is most salubrious, ma'am," she said.

"Oh, healthy, I suppose," said the Grand Duchess with a dismissive wave of her hand, "and it has made you hardy and long-lived, no doubt. But it is mighty disagreeable, nonetheless." She looked at Chastity. "Are you enjoying your stay in London?"

"Very much, ma'am," said Chastity, startled to be asked such a question by a woman who had only been in the country for a few weeks.

"Good!" said the Grand Duchess. "Take advantage of it. It is a city that has much to offer. As all of you have no doubt read in your papers, I have visited your Parliament. Extraordinary institution. How did you find it?"

"I have not visited it, ma'am," said Chastity.

"An oversight," said the Grand Duchess severely. To Lady Trentower: "You must rectify it, and see that the girl spends some time in your Parliament."

Lady Trentower was astonished into silence by this chastisement. Before she could recover the Grand Duchess leaped to another topic, and said to Charles, "I wish to thank you, sir, for the service you rendered to our dear friend—and thus to me—by arranging for her trip to Oxford next week. She is going as a scout for me. I have studied your Parliament, and now I mean to study your universities." She stated this with a saving glint of self-mockery.

"It is an honor to be of service to you both, ma'am," said Charles.

"I hope you will accompany Lady Grasset on her trip?" said the Grand Duchess, watching him carefully.

"We have not discussed the details, ma'am."

"It would give me pleasure to know my dear friend was well cared for," said the Grand Duchess with a commanding stare.

Charles bowed silently.

"Very well," said the Grand Duchess dismissively, "I trust you will enjoy yourselves." She motioned to her left, and such was her authority that the three unquestioningly moved in that direction.

"She is very high-handed," said Lady Trentower.

"She is autocratic," said Charles. "I suppose she has been raised to consider no point of view save her own." He made the observation mildly, and without censure.

"She will have to change her manner or she will

not find a welcome here," said Lady Trentower primly. "What's this about Oxford?"

"I have given Lady Grasset some introductions and advice about her pending visit there."

"So you have been seeing her," said Lady Trentower.

Charles did not answer, for the three found themselves facing the woman in question: Lady Grasset, attended by Count Orlanov, stood among a small group who drifted on as they came up.

"Here is my dear sister and niece. And my dear friend," she announced happily to an impassive Count Orlanov, who bowed formally in their direction. "Now the reception is a success."

"It is apparent that success was guaranteed even before our arrival," said Charles. "You have attracted London like a magnet."

"A magnet, as you know, attracts all metal—the ordinary along with the precious," said Lady Grasset, smiling. "You are the latter, of course."

"Thank you," said Lady Trentower forthrightly, as one who has received no more than her due.

"My dear niece," said Lady Grasset to Chastity, "this gathering holds a particular treat in store for you. I will not be so cruel as to make you guess what special gentleman honors us with his presence."

Chastity did not have to guess, for with a sinking feeling she saw Mr. Brockton bear down upon them with hand outstretched in greeting.

"Miss Dalrymple," he said, "Lady Trentower, Mr. Techett." He bowed to each. Though he was formal and correct, there was a hint of giddiness about him that indicated his great joy at being a guest of the Grand Duchess. "What a noble gathering."

"How do you do, sir," said Chastity.

Lady Trentower nodded, her eyes narrowed. "You have not called lately, sir," she said reprovingly.

Mr. Brockton was almost transported by this notice. "An omission that has made me suffer mightily," he said gratefully. "But I shall rectify it, and soon. Tomorrow, if I may?"

"Of course," said Lady Trentower, and looked meaningfully at Chastity. "We shall be home tomorrow, shall we not, my dear?"

"Yes," said Chastity shortly. She turned away from the beaming Mr. Brockton to find herself looking into the glacial blue eyes of Count Orlanov. The effect was as startling as a plunge into a mountain lake; she returned the intense stare for several seconds, long enough to attract attention from the others.

"My dear," said Lady Trentower reprovingly, "we must go and speak to Lady Holland."

She turned back to her aunt and to the arm of Charles Techett which he now extended coldly.

Lady Grasset was the only one of the group who acted as if nothing had happened. With a pretty little moue of disappointment she said, "Please do not abandon me so quickly. I had hoped to find some little corner and have a few minutes' chat."

"Enchanting idea," agreed Mr. Brockton, who had certainly noticed the long look exchanged between Chastity and Count Orlanov but did not know what to make of it. He grinned at Chastity and said, "Is not your young aunt as delightful as your older one, Miss Dalrymple?" Then, realizing that the compliment was not, perhaps, the most graceful, he tried to retreat by bowing to Lady Trentower. "Older only in terms of wisdom, ma'am, not...uh..." He could not bring it off.

Lady Trentower chilled him with a stare. "Older is older, sir. I see no need to embroider the subject."

"Ha, ha," he forced a laugh. "Delightful." Suddenly he looked unhappy.

Lady Grasset patted his arm. "A kind man," she said. Quickly she moved to Chastity's side and took her hand. "We have never had a talk, in spite of the fact that we are relatives. Perhaps we can do so now. How I should enjoy a long chat with you."

Chastity was already suffering from a welter of emotions brought on by the subtle but marked attentions paid her by Charles in the coach, by the following revelation that he had apparently been seeing Lady Grasset on most friendly terms and was likely to travel to Oxford with her, by the unwelcome appearance of an ardent Mr. Brockton and by the almost physical embrace of Count Orlanov's gaze. Her nerves had been honed to a dreadful sensitivity by Lady Trentower's constant admonitions and unrelenting reminders, as if she needed any, that she was in London to find a husband; the fund of confidence she had borne from Grangeford had been quite worn away.

Now, suddenly, her rival, swathed in yards and yards of rustling black silk, came swooping down on her like an amiable fat raven with what seemed an offer of friendship. Chastity was guarded. On the one hand she had no reason to believe that Lady Grasset had at that instant developed a warm feeling for her; on the other hand she had absolutely not one person to whom she could talk intimately, with whom she could share even the smallest portion of her distress. She was a desperate creature under her calm, smiling, controlled facade. Though her reason warned her that she would be foolish to trust Lady Grasset, her instinct dictated that she give way to the woman's blandishments.

"I should be delighted," she said quietly.

"How nice," said Lady Grasset gaily. To the rest she added, "You musn't look for us for some time, mind you, for we have a great deal to discuss. We are, remember, not only relatives, but are also two women—with women's propensity to chatter." Leading Chastity away she said, "Come, we shall go to my rooms."

As they left they were followed by the disapproving stare of Lady Trentower, the coldly indifferent look of Charles Techett, the confused but benign smile of Mr. Brockton, and Count Orlanov's passionate inscrutability.

Chastity strolled arm in arm with Lady Grasset as they passed from the large reception room into the corridor, mounted a stairway and walked down another corridor. They chatted about the weather, the location of the hotel ("Very convenient for the Grand Duchess..."), the furnishings ("Ordinary but serviceable...") and finally they arrived at a door, which Lady Grasset opened; she stepped aside to allow Chastity to enter.

Even in the dim light of the rainy day Chastity could see that the room was exquisitely furnished. It was a sort of sitting room and library, for there was a desk and a cluster of little chairs around the grate in which a small fire burned, and a chaise longue near one of the windows. Every object was delicately crafted: the furniture was light and graceful, the Persian carpet glowed red and blue, and blue satin drapes hung at the windows. The vases filled with tulips were the most enchanting Sèvres, and crystal candlesticks and sconces gleamed. Oil paintings in gilt frames hung on the wall. The air of casual elegance and luxury contrasted so sharply with the pedestrian corridor beyond that the room seemed part of another, much grander building. Lady Grasset touched a taper to the fire and lit several candles while she continued recounting tales of the long trip from Saint Petersburg. She indicated a chair near the grate, and took one herself.

"What a lovely room," said Chastity looking around. "I had no idea the appointments here would be so agreeable."

Lady Grasset laughed. "They are not, generally. All this," she waved carelessly around her, "I brought myself." She paused and smiled. "Everything here was a gift from my late husband." The remark was made without any affectation; certainly it was devoid of sentiment. "Of course," she continued, "the real gift he gave me was the ability to appreciate the objects. He taught me how to enjoy beauty." She spoke dispassionately, almost indifferently; she might have been describing someone else.

The tenor of her remarks and her manner of delivering them were so at odds with her previous conversation that Chastity was momentarily disoriented. Lady Grasset appeared to have taken on a different personality, as though she had been transformed by the room. The only reply Chastity could muster was, "How very fine for you."

"Yes," said Lady Grasset, choosing to interpret the remark as if it had been a considered observation. "It was indeed very fine for me. He took an uneducated and unrefined girl and made of her someone who could appreciate all this." Again she waved carelessly around the room. "In addition, he made certain that I would be able to afford to indulge my new and rarefied tastes by leaving me sufficient money. That is another of his gifts, one he continues to lavish from beyond the grave."

Chastity was embarrassed by this sudden plunge into intimacy. In spite of herself she assumed a prim disapproving air to ward off further confidences, much as a farmer will raise a fence to keep rabbits out.

Lady Grasset noticed, but chose to leap the fence. "Of course, one of the things Lord Grasset could not change was my basic nature, which is rather too open and forthright to mesh easily with the manners of society. I *can* restrain my opinions and feelings, but I don't enjoy it; I feel as though my soul were corseted. So I occasionally erupt, burst out of my bonds and indulge myself in unguarded expression—as I am doing now, I fear, much to your consternation."

"Not at all," said Chastity stiffly, a set smile on her face.

Lady Grasset shrugged good humoredly. "I can go just so long babbling the sort of nonsense that will offend no one, and then I must find relief. It struck me just now, when I saw you lock eyes with Peter, that possibly you also needed some sort of respite."

Chastity prepared to feign incomprehension; her eyebrows were already lifted in simulated surprise and there was the trace of a quizzical smile on her lips as though she could not imagine what Lady Grasset was alluding to. This would have been the sensible course to follow. Then her desolation and confusion swamped her good sense, and she said, "I was not aware my exchange with Count Orlanov was so noticeable."

"It was, to all of us gathered around you. I would have noticed—have noticed, I must say—any communication because I have been aware of the attraction between you. Whether your aunt and Charles shared my knowledge I cannot say. I suspect they do now. I am, however, fairly certain that Mr. Brockton remains unenlightened."

"If you were aware... then Count Orlanov must have confided in you." Chastity stated this flatly, like a barrister arranging his arguments.

"No, no, no," said Lady Grasset, laughing. "If you think Peter is capable of such a breach you know him less well then I thought. Never, by one word, has he *directly* indicated to me that he is enamoured of you."

"Then..."

"How did I know? I have eyes, have I not? Your little *tête à tête*'s—particularly in your aunt's drawing room—had a significance for me that would escape others. Also, Peter has indicated, in the most tactful and gentlemanly way, that he would be relieved by a cessation of our liaison." Lady Grasset's eyes shone with worldly amusement, as though she were sharing a joke.

"So you are... have been..."

"We are still lovers, at least formally. Peter's

sense of honor is such that he would be incapable of terminating our arrangement unless I agreed. In fact," Lady Grasset added, her eyes amused again, "his sense of honor is so strong that he dare not ask to be excused. He can barely bring himself to hint. He is waiting for me to set him free."

"He must respect you very much to be so delicate."

"Yes, we have grown to respect each other over the years. But actually his delicacy is as much a tribute to his sense of obligation to my late husband as to me."

"Obligation? Was Lord Grasset aware..."

"Aware? It was he who arranged the matter." Lady Grasset smiled straightforwardly, without any hint of brazenness or apology. Her attitude was of one who is stating an interesting and amusing fact.

"I see," said Chastity, though she most decidedly did not. She felt she should disapprove, but Lady Grasset was so forthright and good-natured that any show of censure would have seemed ill-mannered.

"I am not exposing any secrets," said Lady Grasset with a shrug. "The story is well known in Saint Petersburg—at least to those whose opinion matters. The Grand Duchess, for example, has been aware of our arrangement since its inception." She looked thoughtfully into the glowing grate. "I am not eager for the details to be divulged here in England. But I don't know you well enough to ask for secrecy, so I must take the consequences of my reckless tongue." She laughed ruefully.

"I can assure you of my discretion," said Chastity.

"That is very kind," said Lady Grasset rather ironically. She continued to study the fire for a few seconds, while the rain pelted the windows. She shifted her bulk in the delicate chair and smiled at Chastity. "Even before we came to London I was aware that the situation between Peter and myself would have to change, and equally aware that because of the delicacy of his nature the incentive would have to come from me. It was very complicated, though, for I could not simply say, 'It is finished.' That would have been uncivil. There had to be some extraneous reason for the termination. You, it appears, are that reason." She shrugged again. "One pays a high price in complications for refinement of feelings."

Chastity did not know what to say, for she was utterly confused. She could not imagine what kind of arrangement Lady Grasset was discussing—it was foreign to everything in her experience. She kept an interested, bland look on her face, as she said again, "I see."

Lady Grasset glanced at her sharply, then smiled into the fire. "I do not think you do," she said with a little laugh. "Why should you? Why should anyone? I daresay that the mélange of temperaments—Lord Grasset's, mine and Peter's—have created an unusual arrangement. You met your uncle, my late husband, when we visited Grangeford. What did you think of him?" Her question was posed in an interested, mild conversational tone.

"I remember him as being gracious and accomplished. He seemed kind."

"And me? What did you think of me?"

Chastity looked into the grate, and did not answer immediately.

"I have embarrassed you," said Lady Grasset, smiling. "I do that to people. It's a demon that possesses me. I cannot help myself, it seems. I am sorry. But I am also very curious. What *did* you think of me when I passed through Grangeford?"

The fire in the grate, the glow of candles in dim daylight, the rain pelting the windows, the exquisitely furnished room, and above all Lady Grasset's unexpected revelations, both of information and of character—all conspired to reduce Chastity's reserve. Under other circumstances she would have replied that she thought Lady Grasset had been very nice. Now she looked at her and said, "I thought you were tragic."

Lady Grasset lifted her brows, not so much in surprise as with interest. "Why?"

"I knew that you were being separated from Mr. Techett, and that you were a girl—you were scarcely twenty, I think—a girl without any means of support or family. When my uncle declared he was going to marry you I wanted to save you from him in spite of the fact that he appeared to be as good and kind as any man could be. I still remember your departure from Grangeford vividly: I urged you to stay, and not go to Russia. You looked at me as though I had taken leave of my senses." Chastity smiled in reminiscence.

Lady Grasset smiled also—a good-natured, pleasant smile. "Strange," she said. "I don't remember any of that. Certainly, I cannot recall an effort by anyone to 'save' me." She tilted her head to one side, and added, "To disrupt my marriage to Lord Grasset would not have been my salvation, you know. On the contrary, it would have been the ruin of me. If he had not married me, he would have made me his mistress—and where would I be now?" She looked around her room. "Not sitting here, a friend of the Grand Duchess and surrounded by artifacts, any one of which cost more than I was able to earn in a year before I married your uncle."

"I thought that your love for Mr. Techett should have been honored."

"Correctly so," said Lady Grasset. "It was very sincere and quite passionate. But it could not last. No emotions as potent as those I entertained for Charles could have survived for very long."

"Then you are no longer interested in him?" asked Chastity.

"I did not say that. On the contrary, I find him very appealing. But both he and I are different people now, and my attraction is a different sort entirely from what it was ten years ago."

"I see," said Chastity, and this time she did. She turned melancholy.

Lady Grasset studied her for a moment before shifting in her chair again and saying, "But we were talking about my marriage to your uncle. I do not wish to make Lord Grasset sound immoral or callous. He was neither of those things. He was an extremely kind man; your impression was correct. He was also extraordinarily sensitive to his physical surroundings. His taste was exquisite. That was why he chose to marry me when Charles had to shed me in order to take on a rich wife; he married me because I was the most beautiful woman in London." Lady Grasset stated this in such a matter of fact way that it was impossible to accuse her of conceit; she was simply stating a fact. She was neither proud nor apologetic. "Such was his refinement, however, that it overshadowed some of his other qualities; threw some of his inclinations out of balance, so to speak." She paused, and smoothed her skirt thoughtfully.

"Because I was barely twenty years of age," she continued, "and he was past sixty, he was certain I would take a lover. He was resigned to this, even though I assured him I was not a woman who entered into liaisons lightly, and that I was quite content to honor my marital vows to him. I believe I was speaking the truth, although who can say what would have happened had he not taken matters in hand.

"What he did was choose my lover for me, just as he chose my clothes, my art, my vases, my furniture. After three years of marriage he chose Count Orlanov, not only because he considered his appearance as very nicely complementing my own—the combination of Peter's blonde handsomeness and my brunette beauty pleased him—but also because he found Peter's character to be excellent. He enjoyed, he said, seeing us together. I believe him."

Chastity was at a loss for words for a few seconds. She regarded Lady Grasset's rotund face, and had to make an effort to keep her jaw from going slack. Finally she said, "But Count Orlanov? Did he agree so easily? He does not seem..."

"He does not seem like the sort who could be maneuvered into an affair? He was not." Lady Grasset sighed. "I fear that what I'm going to say will put Peter in a bad light—but you must not judge him by your own standards.

"Peter comes from a very fine family—not one of the most exalted of the nobility, nor one of the most ancient, but fine, nonetheless. Unfortunately a profligate grandparent had spent the family into very hard times. They were exceedingly poor when my husband intervened. There were two daughters and Peter, and a rather retiring mother and a quite incompetent father. Peter was sent to Saint Petersburg to work as some minor aide, but his extraordinary looks quickly brought him to the attention of the court.

"Lord Grasset learned of his background and his family's distress. Very delicately—as delicate as only he could be—he approached the Orlanovs with his proposal: he would provide the daughters with dowries, and would see to the comfort of the elder Orlanovs, and in addition would settle a handsome sum on Peter. I doubt if he ever exactly specified just what Peter had to do to earn this munificence—but everyone understood.

"So you see," said Lady Grasset with a little sigh of amused resignation, "your uncle bought Peter for me just as he bought all of this." She motioned around the room once more.

"But... but there must have been gossip..." said Chastity, as confounded by the fact she was having this conversation as by the story Lady Grasset was telling her.

"There is always gossip," said Lady Grasset with a shrug. "No one, however, knew the exact details of the arrangement. It was obvious when Peter became my lover, but none of us—Lord Grasset, the Orlanovs or myself—was foolish enough to spread the particulars through society. But you're right; there was gossip. There was gossip, though, before Peter became my lover, as there was bound to be about a sixty-year-old husband with a twenty-year-old wife. What Lord Grasset did was to make sure that he was cuckolded by someone who was worthy of me—and of himself.

"Little by little the details came out—mostly, I fear, because of my unfortunate inability to keep a secret. I have, as you can see, a dreadful need to explain myself." She made a mock-helpless gesture. "But by the time the whole story was known, everyone was accustomed to seeing the three of us together—my husband, my lover and me—and there was little more than a few raised eyebrows. No one has ever been rude to me. I doubt if Peter has suffered. If anything was said to Lord Grasset he never let on; I don't think he would have been bothered, for he was quite philosophical."

Chastity nodded with what she hoped was a noncensurious look. She did not actually condemn the arrangement Lady Grasset described, nor did she at that moment feel any differently toward the participants. She knew, however, that such behavior flouted all conventional rules of relationships, and consequently she felt that it behooved her to disapprove. In the light of her own limited experience in the area of human intercourse—that vast sea that Lady Grasset seemed to have charted so interestingly—she had little to offer by way of comment except, "It is evident that the plan has benefited all who took part in it." She spoke with a determinedly pleasant tone of voice, as one might commend a child for a task well done.

If Lady Grasset noticed her condescension she did not react to it. Instead, she shrugged good-naturedly and said, "My husband gained peace of mind because he was cuckolded by someone he considered both aesthetically and socially worthy of me; Peter, of course, saved his family and improved his own fortune. I, however, gained nothing." She smiled ironically. "I did not want a lover when one was foisted on me. Even though the intentions of my husband were kind, and might have been interpreted to be in my best interests, I realize now that I resented it horribly when Peter was introduced to our home. Not, I hasten to add, because I was awash in love for Lord Grasset; I was not. But I respected him, and would have been quite content simply to be his wife. I am not a particularly passionate woman, and had no need for the attentions of a young man."

Chastity blushed and looked at the fire with concentration. Lady Grasset chose not to notice. "But I was given no say in the matter. So I set about making my protest in my own way. I began to eat."

Chastity was not sure she had heard correctly. She looked at Lady Grasset quickly to ascertain whether she was serious.

Her quizzical look was returned with the same good-humored expression Lady Grasset had worn during the whole strange interview. "I do not mean that I consciously set out to revenge myself; but now, after several years have passed—and many pounds have been gained—I wonder.... No, I don't wonder; I know, that in my heart, if not in my head, I decided to do this." She made a gesture with both hands beginning at her shoulders and swooping down her enormous front. "I began to eat and eat and eat." She smiled. "I always had a tendency to gain weight, and had always been careful, since a good figure was essential to my beauty, and hence to my position in the world. This fat you see is my revenge for having been treated as an object that was in the eyes of Lord Grasset no less—and, I suspect, no more—precious than his paintings, vases and carpets. I saw to it that his acquisition of me, at least, did not remain a source of pride and enjoyment." She laughed without bitterness, throwing her head back in a charming, girlish gesture of amusement. "Wasn't that wicked of me?" she asked naughtily.

Chastity was nonplussed. "I . . . I would not presume to judge . . ." she said, then cleared her throat and began again, "I certainly cannot judge your behavior. I am sure you had sufficient provocation, at least according to your own lights." She paused before adding, "Ultimately, you have harmed no one save yourself."

"Ah," said Lady Grasset, "that is not true. I believe I harmed my husband, although he never once, by word or deed, intimated that he was distressed at my amplitude. Never did he suggest I forgo a pastry or do without a refreshment. Never did he allude to my size; and when I did, for I was always calling attention to my figure, he said nothing, but would smile without rancor or accusation. Lord Grasset was the most consummate gentleman I have ever met." She sighed and looked at the fire. There was no sentimentality in her tone or gesture, but rather a melancholy appreciation.

After a few seconds she brightened and turned to Chastity. "You see how incorrigible I am! I have told you my whole life, and have not given you the opportunity to say a thing. Now that I have unburdened myself—and how pent up I have been since I came to London!—I can address your situation with all my attention." She smiled winningly. "Tell me, who is it you intend to marry?"

Chapter Eight

Chastity was appalled at the sudden shift of focus from Lady Grasset to herself. Though she sat as still as before, and her expression remained as politely attentive, she suffered an attack of panic as Lady Grasset's large dark eyes turned on her with their glowing concern.

Chastity had listened to the bizarre account of the woman's marriage—it seemed uncomfortably like a confession—with mounting unease, for people simply did not discuss themselves with so little restraint. While Lady Grasset was talking, Chastity had made allowances for her: The woman had been born into deprived circumstances, she had been married to a man much older than herself, she had spent the last decade in a strange and barbaric country where heaven only knew what social usages prevailed. For each revelation Lady Grasset had exhumed, Chastity had silently countered with one or another extenuating condition.

Now, it appeared, Lady Grasset was demanding from her the same untrammeled disclosures. Chastity could not furnish them; not only was she too well-bred to indulge in such confidences, there was nothing in her background of sufficient scope and weight to balance Lady Grasset's experience.

Lady Grasset's question, "Tell me, who is it you

intend to marry?" hung heavily in the air, while Chastity retained her small pleasant smile, and kept her hands folded neatly in her lap; her stomach was churning.

"I really have no intentions..." she began.

Lady Grasset fanned the air with a graceful wave of her hand. "'Intend' was the wrong word, I suppose. More simply, who do you want to marry?"

"I am not at all sure who, or even if, I wish to marry."

"Ah?" said Lady Grasset with a lift of her brow. "I had the impression you were quite ready to take a spouse."

"Even if that were the case, I have received no proposal."

Lady Grasset raised her eyebrow further. "Perhaps not in so many words, but surely it is evident that Mr. Brockton favors you. Also, it is incontestable that Peter is pursuing you. Perhaps neither of these gentlemen has been sufficiently explicit, but surely there can be no question of their intentions." She looked closely at Chastity.

"I don't really know either of those gentlemen very well," said Chastity stiffly, hoping to terminate the conversation with this show of reticence.

Lady Grasset was not deflected. "I can certainly help you there," she said with a delighted laugh; at the same time there was a mischievous glint in her eyes. "Though I have only met Mr. Brockton recently, my intuition is that he is a solid, honest gentleman who would do his best to content the wife of his choice. I honestly believe that if I were in the market for a husband, I should set my cap for Mr. Brockton. I hope I don't make you jealous?"

Chastity responded with a small smile, but said nothing.

"As for Peter... well, I can tell you a great deal about Peter. He is an innocent, in many ways, an impetuous, chivalrous, strong-hearted innocent."

Chastity could not contain a start of surprise at this description.

Lady Grasset laughed. "I know that his appearance leads one to believe he must be quite devilish, and a veritable rake. He is not. He is attentive, kind and honorable."

"No doubt..."

"You hesitate because he took money from my husband for what many would consider a peculiar, or even reprehensible, task. I do hope you will not hold this fact against Peter; you would be doing him a grave disservice if you did. How many men could you name who would feel bound to continue such a bargain even after the money had been received and the benefactor who had paid it had died?"

"None," Chastity replied quite truthfully.

"I daresay not," said Lady Grasset, "Peter continues as my cavalier, I assure you, simply because he gave his word to my husband. Nothing else keeps him by my side. Absolutely nothing."

"Do you mean he no longer... uh..."

"He is no longer my lover. His performance in that capacity, furthermore, was most perfunctory. Neither of us was particularly taken with the other. We were two very beautiful dolls, or mannequins, thrown together to satisfy the refined taste of Lord Grasset. Peter has faithfully—so far as I know—paraded by my side these last eight or so years, in spite of the fact he has never really loved me. So, if he is smitten with you, I daresay you are his first love." Lady Grasset's large face expanded further in a friendly smile. "I suppose, though, you will disappoint him," she added.

"How so?"

"Why, surely you would not marry him?"

Chastity was surprised at the finality of Lady Grasset's tone. "You have just defended his conduct most enthusiastically, and have given him an excellent character. Why do you assume I would not accept your evaluation?"

"Conduct and character!" said Lady Grasset, tossing her head, and placing her hand on her large bosom. "Those aren't the ingredients one looks for in a spouse. One looks for compatibility—that is, if one is wise, as I'm sure you are. I can't imagine that you and Peter would remain congenial towards each other for very long."

"Why not?" asked Chastity testily.

Lady Grasset became pensive. "Peter is from a milieu that is much different from yours. He is accustomed to the protocol and splendor of court. This is his first voyage away from that setting, and no doubt he finds this country, and its inhabitants—including you—exotic. I fear, though, that if he were to stay he would become disenchanted. And, of course, I realize it would be out of the question for you to go to Saint Petersburg with him. For you, I realize, he is a delectable conquest in passing, but impossible to consider for a lifetime."

Chastity flushed with anger. She controlled her voice, though her eyes were narrowed. "I think you are assuming too much, both about me and about Count Orlanov."

"I think not," said Lady Grasset, smiling evenly. "But no matter. I am sure you are much too sensible to do something foolish. If Peter persists in his courtship, I have every faith in your ability to steer him toward more reasonable behavior."

Chastity rose abruptly. "Whether it has been your intention or not, you have insulted me."

Lady Grasset got to her feet with all the alacrity her majestic bulk would permit. There was consternation and sympathy in her voice as she said, "My dear, my dear, I assure you nothing could have been further from my mind. What did I say that has so unnerved you?"

Chastity regretted her outburst immediately, all the more so as she was faced with trying to explain it. What so incensed her was that she had been called sensible and reasonable, two attributes most would accept as compliments. Chastity, however, equated the traits with dullness and predictability, the very quintessence of what she was trying to escape. It was impossible to articulate this to Lady Grasset, who hovered near her with genuine concern. Instead, after a pause, she said, "Forgive me, but I am very taut. I . . ."

"Say no more," said Lady Grasset, with a gentle pat on her shoulder. "Though I have never undergone a season of husband hunting, I can well imagine the strain such an undertaking imposes."

Chastity sighed with resignation. Try as she might, there was no way she could escape the label of husband hunter. If it had not been accurate she would have been amused. Since, however, it was all too apt, she was distressed each time the subject was mentioned. She decided, though, not to deny it any further to Lady Grasset, as this would only prolong a conversation that was making her increasingly uncomfortable. Since both she and Lady Grasset were on their feet, Chastity assumed they would be returning to the reception below.

Lady Grasset, however, was not ready to abandon their conversation. She sat again, and motioned Chastity to do the same, and without allowing a demurrer, she said, "One way to ease your anxiety is to determine upon a plan of action. You say you have received no proposals. What you mean, of course, is that you have not received *the* proposal that would make you happy. We must set about correcting this deficiency."

Chastity sat gingerly on the edge of her chair to show she was poised for instant departure, and that this was to be only the briefest coda to their discussion.

"What we must do is bring Mr. Brockton to the point," continued Lady Grasset.

"That is precisely what I must not do," said Chastity coldly. "I have endeavored, with all my abilities, to keep Mr. Brockton from coming to the point, as you put it. I have had to exercise considerable ingenuity to prevent his making a proposal."

"Why should you follow such a course?" asked Lady Grasset, intrigued. It was obvious she thought Chastity had outlined some devious plan, and was interested in the workings of it.

"Because I do not wish to marry him."

After an instant's silence Lady Grasset said, "But he would be perfect for you."

Chastity expelled a great and exasperated sigh.

"I am weary of hearing that Mr. Brockton would be a suitable husband for me. I do not dislike Mr. Brockton. He is an honorable gentleman. He is considerate and, no doubt, kind. But I do not wish to marry him."

Gently prodding, Lady Grasset said, "Can you not tell me what your objections are?"

"He has no dash," said Chastity immediately, without even thinking. She looked defiantly at Lady Grasset and repeated, "Mr. Brockton has no dash."

"I see." Lady Grasset was thoughtful. "Peter has dash, and to spare," she said, watching Chastity carefully.

"That...is true."

"Is that the criterion you are seeking in a spouse, then—dash?"

"No, of course not. Or rather, that is not the only qualification. But..."

"But you would not like to confer your hand on a man who was lacking it?"

"No."

Lady Grasset stared at the fire with pursed lips. "Personally, I do not find Mr. Brockton dull."

"People are not urging you to marry him."

"That is true. Well, this puts a new light on the matter." Lady Grasset solemnly shook her head from side to side and said, "I fear I must reiterate that, dash or no dash, I do not believe you and Peter would be a good match." She looked unhappy.

Chastity stood again, with determination. "This matter need not concern you. I appreciate your interest and your advice—for I recognize you offer both in a spirit of kindness—but I assure you I am capable of arriving at a decision concerning my own future alone."

Lady Grasset did not stand, nor appear to notice that Chastity was attempting to terminate the conversation. "There is, of course, a third possibility, one we have not yet mentioned."

Impatiently Chastity looked toward the door and wished she had already passed through it.

Ignoring her gesture Lady Grasset said, simply, "Charles Techett."

In order to discourage this peculiar meddling Chastity made her expression blank, but Lady Grasset was not deterred. "Charles Techett," she repeated in a ruminative tone, all the while watching Chastity speculatively. "I noticed that he was conferring a rather flirtatious attention on you. Frankly though, I did not give the matter much consideration. Charles, of course, would be even less appropriate for you than Peter."

Chastity drew herself up to full height. "You are not a suitable judge of that," she said.

Lady Grasset shrugged. "On the contrary. I know Charles very well, and not only because of our former liaison."

With a sharp look at Lady Grasset, Chastity wondered again whether she and Charles had recommenced their intimacy. She felt jealousy. "I cannot speak about your acquaintance with Mr. Techett. That is beyond my purview. I can, however, state with absolute certainty that you are not in a position to evaluate me and my capabilities. I cannot take umbrage at your attempt to do so, because I am convinced you are acting out of good will. But I must ask you to desist, for your knowledge of me is too superficial to allow such intimacy."

Lady Grasset nodded several times, as though Chastity had just confirmed some insight. Then, with a rueful smile, she said, "Of course, you are correct. I do not know you well. And I have no wish to force myself into a closeness you find obnoxious. I shall certainly desist from trying to influence you, and at the same time ask you to forgive my... abandon. As I said earlier, I have an unfortunate tendency toward unguarded expression. When I go for too long without speaking my thoughts I erupt into frankness. That is what I have just done, and I have distressed you. I hope you will forgive me."

Her request was made so prettily that Chastity would have felt surly had she not immediately given her assurance. "Please. There is nothing to forgive. I spoke more sharply than I intended." Impulsively she held out her hand.

Lady Grasset squeezed it warmly. "Ah, well, I suppose we must return to the reception," she said, rising. "Our little conversation has done me a world of good. I'm sorry it should have caused you discomfort."

She opened the door to the corridor and stepped back for Chastity to pass. Then, after closing the door she took her arm and they began to wander the way they had come. Lady Grasset, without any apparent effort, fell into the meaningless patter that had accompanied their stroll to her quarters. There was no attempt to elicit a response, nor even to make a great deal of sense; her talk was very much like the subdued string music played in drawing rooms after dinner. One could listen or not; it was not obtrusive.

Chastity listened with only half an ear, for she was thinking over Lady Grasset's statement during her burst of intimacy, that she knew Charles Techett very well indeed, and not only because of their former liaison. She supposed, with a stronger twinge of jealousy, that they had rekindled their feelings for each other. Why, then, had Charles Techett made such advances to her? Was it possible that he was merely flirting? Passing the time? It pained her to think so. Even more hurtful was the idea that he might have been paying attention to her in order to disguise his interest in Lady Grasset—that he had used her as a distraction. She shook off that thought, but another took its place: Just what had Lady Grasset meant when she had insisted that Charles Techett was not for her? Why was he not for her? She found it hard to believe that Charles Techett was harboring some shameful secret; so far as she knew, Lady Grasset was the only scandal in his past, and that one, certainly, was in the open. Could it have been that Lady Grasset meant that he was too dissimilar to her, that, like Count Orlanov, his background made him incompatible? Chastity clenched her jaw at this possibility. If that interpretation was correct Lady Grasset was saying, in effect, that Chastity was too much of a provincial, a country girl, for the worldly and sophisticated Charles. As her bulky and loquacious companion chattered on, Chastity injected an "Oh?" or a "Really?" from time to time, but she began to seethe. When they had arrived back in the large room, arm in arm, and to all appearances, on the most amiable terms,

Chastity felt more hostile toward Lady Grasset than ever.

The crowd was denser than when they had left, and the components of it more brilliant. The rain, rather than discouraging gaiety, had brought the guests together in a glistening circle of light picked out of the damp atmosphere beyond the tall windows of the Pulteney Hotel. The conversation was animated yet genteely subdued, so there was only a hum and not a hubbub. At the far end of the room the Grand Duchess still sat on her improvised throne, before which a man and woman were listening with attention as the small woman held forth, all the while casting her lively dark eyes this way and that to make certain her fete was proceeding as she wished.

With a raised hand she summoned Lady Grasset, who gracefully sailed through the crowd with Chastity on her arm while saying, "The Grand Duchess is talking to the Russian ambassador, Count Lieven, and his wife. He is very nice, but she is proud. Perhaps you know them?"

"No," said Chastity, uninterested. Her one thought was to escape Lady Grasset's smothering attention, find her aunt and leave the reception.

"Well, then, you must meet them, for whatever her faults she is very grand and is intimate with anyone of importance," Lady Grasset dropped her voice, "including the Prince Regent."

By this time they had reached the Grand Duchess, who acknowledged their arrival with an expansive gesture of welcome, and the Lievens, who regarded them both with masks of detached politeness.

"Here is my social arbiter, my English bellwether," said the Grand Duchess with a malicious little laugh. The Lievens became stiffer, and their smiles, already small and rigid, became even more fixed.

"Lady Grasset," said Count Lieven, bowing over her hand. Countess Lieven favored her with a barely perceptible nod.

Lady Grasset appeared to notice no slight. Her large face glowed with good humor and she broke into a little peal of pleased laughter. "How happy it always makes me to see you," she said, and Chastity could have sworn she was telling the truth. "I am all the more delighted at this meeting, because it gives me the opportunity to present my niece, Chastity Dalrymple."

The count bowed over Chastity's hand, murmuring that he was enchanted. Countess Lieven studied her with an expression that came close to showing distaste; her lips were crimped and her nose pinched. Her eyes were glacial. "Delighted," she said in a tight, cold voice.

Her response seemed to amuse the Grand Duchess. With malice peeking through a mock innocent smile she said to the countess, "You must be sure to have Miss Dalrymple at your next reception. I hear they are famous among the ton of this city, and Miss Dalrymple will be an attraction."

Countess Lieven bowed to the Grand Duchess and said, "It will give me great pleasure to see Miss Dalrymple in our home." Never, Chastity thought, had she heard tone so at variance with words.

"Splendid," said the Grand Duchess. "Now I must ask my dear friend and adviser just what course to follow in this matter of entertaining the little Princess Charlotte." Her smile was feline. "Count Lieven and his wife tell me it would be a grave mistake to cultivate the daughter of the Prince Regent, since at the moment daughter and father are having a little dispute about who the daughter is to marry. I, on the other hand, think that if a daughter is being bullied by her papa into marrying an oaf, she needs friendship more than ever. It is my wish to offer whatever support I can to the little princess. Do you not think that wise, my friend?" she asked Lady Grasset.

"One can never err while being kind," said Lady Grasset with her most open and guileless smile.

Count Lieven, with pained affability, said, "The matter is not so simple as that. If your highness interferes in this dispute between a sovereign and his daughter you could be accused of meddling in affairs of state. This would be regarded a grave insult in some quarters."

The Grand Duchess shrugged. "What do I care how I'm regarded 'in some quarters'? My heart goes out to the poor child. I shall follow my dear friend's advice and be kind. You are right," she added, turning to Lady Grasset with a show of ironic piety, "one can never err when one is being kind."

Both the Lievens resumed their masks of diplomatic politeness, though the countess had some difficulty in completely subduing her annoyance.

The Grand Duchess turned to her and said sweetly, "Am I not correct, countess?"

"Most certainly, your highness," Countess Lieven replied evenly. She put her hand on her husband's arm and both of them took a rigidly formal leave of the little group.

"I have put a few noses out of joint," said the Grand Duchess affably.

"I fear, ma'am, that both of them, and particularly *she*, will hold this against you," said Lady Grasset noncommittally.

The Grand Duchess laughed. "Let them. If they cause trouble I shall have my brother recall them. Nothing is simpler." She looked around the room with satisfaction. "Perhaps they have been in England too long, as it is."

Chastity, who had watched the little drama while standing to one side, reflected that it would be exceedingly unpleasant to be at the mercy of the Grand Duchess and in her bad graces. She felt a surge of respect for the apparently artless tact Lady Grasset had to exercise to keep on the good side of the despotic little woman. At the same time she could not help feeling that the continuing effort was somewhat despicable.

Her rumination was cut short by the Grand Duchess's next remark. "I must admit that the countess does have very good connections, both here and abroad. She will be invaluable to us in Vienna."

Chastity paid close attention as Lady Grasset replied, "There is no question that you are correct, ma'am."

The Grand Duchess looked over their heads. "There is Lord Castelreagh. I was wondering whether to be insulted if he did not come." She smiled with both triumph and coquetry as the English prime minister approached. Lady Grasset, keeping Chastity on her arm, retreated in order to allow them privacy.

As soon as they had receded a sufficient distance from the platform to avoid being overheard, Chastity asked, "Are you going to Vienna?"

Lady Grasset raised her shoulders expressively. "*Everyone* is going to Vienna," she said, in the offhand way one might announce that simply everyone was going to be at a certain ball or rout.

"I was not aware of that," said Chastity. "When will this be?"

"In a few months. Perhaps sooner. There is to be a congress of nations to discuss the peace now that Napoleon has been defeated."

Chastity was not so interested in the implications of the meeting in Vienna as in the information that Lady Grasset would be leaving London. "In a few months," however, seemed very far away on this rainy April afternoon.

Even the small lift of spirits that Chastity experienced was dispelled when Lady Grasset added, "But who knows what could happen between now and then. I might very well decide not to go." She was nonchalant, the plaything of circumstances. With a surge of anger Chastity abruptly removed her hand from the woman's arm. Lady Grasset was surprised, but had not time to inquire as to her reasons, for Lady Trentower and Joseph Brockton bore down on them.

"There you are," said Lady Trentower accusingly. "I had become quite worried. I thought you must have left alone. You have been gone for a very long time." She directed her remarks solely to Chastity.

Lady Grasset answered. "I am to blame. Please forgive me, dear sister, for spiriting your companion away. But after all, she is my niece, also, and I did so enjoy getting to know her better."

"Fortunate girl that you are, Miss Dalrymple, to have two such aunts!" said Mr. Brockton. His exclamation was not the sort to encourage discussion, and he was ignored.

"Did you wish to leave?" Chastity asked her aunt.

"Leave? So soon?" Lady Trentower glanced around the crowded room, checking any overlooked possibilities. "Well, I suppose we might." She turned to Mr. Brockton. "Summon Mr. Techett, if you'd be so kind, and tell him we shall be leaving." She paused before adding, "If, of course, it is his pleasure to do so."

"Alas for our poor reception," said Lady Grasset with a pretty show of distress. "Almost everyone of interest is leaving." She turned to Mr. Brockton. "I do hope, sir, that you will not desert me also."

Mr. Brockton's ebullience at being so singled out by the dearest friend of the Grand Duchess was tempered by his awareness that a too great display of joy at the honor might well mean retribution from Lady Trentower. He quelled his impulse to return a lavish compliment, and settled for a murmured, "I am at your service, ma'am." Then he went off to search for Charles Techett.

"A very worthy gentleman," said Lady Trentower as he left. She looked sharply at Chastity, ready to counter whatever objections she might make to the statement.

Chastity did not respond, but Lady Grasset said, "He is the quintessence of an English gentleman. So sturdy, so honest." She and Lady Trentower exchanged approving glances while Chastity looked around the room.

Her eyes fell on Count Orlanov who was standing several paces behind Lady Trentower and Lady Grasset, and out of sight of both of them. He was staring at her fixedly, his body at rigid attention, his expression harshly passionate. He was extremely handsome, Chastity thought; she had never seen such a handsome man. He made no effort to approach, but kept his eyes locked on her.

"Charles," said Lady Trentower, "we were thinking of leaving."

Charles Techett had approached unnoticed by Chastity. As she turned to him from Count Orlanov's impassioned regard, she saw he had noticed the direction of her attention. His face was closed, but the eyes were supercilious as they flicked across the space between her and the count. "If you're quite sure you're ready, I shall be happy to accompany you," he said with a small sarcastic smile. He pointedly ignored Chastity.

"Yes, I think we can leave," said Lady Trentower, her investigation of the premises complete. To Lady Grasset she said grudgingly, "The reception has been a success. Your Grand Duchess has attracted a very creditable crowd, considering that the season has not yet even begun." She did not look pleased.

"How could it be anything but a success with guests such as you to grace it," said Lady Grasset winningly, as she smiled at all of them.

Lady Trentower nodded her head in thoughtful agreement. "Give me your arm," she said to Charles. "Goodbye." She nodded to Lady Grasset and Mr. Brockton. Chastity smiled a formal farewell and took Charles's free arm. As the three of them walked toward the exit Lady Trentower suddenly stopped and said, "I must speak to Mrs.

Brougham. Proceed without me. I shall not be a moment, and shall find you at the carriage." She shot off in another direction, leaving Charles and Chastity in sudden and unwelcome intimacy.

They progressed through the crowd, out the door and down the stairs without saying a word. Charles instructed a footman to summon his carriage, then stood, solid, straight, impervious, looking off into an invisible distance. Chastity cleared her throat twice before saying, "The weather does not seem to have deterred anyone."

"No."

"Of course, one doesn't know who would have come if there had been sunshine. Perhaps the crowd would have been larger." She began to feel inane, and to admire Lady Grasset's ability to chatter endlessly about nothing.

"Yes."

"But then, if the weather had been splendid I suppose it is possible that many who came here would have found other diversions."

"That's possible."

Chastity capitulated. She could say nothing more in the face of Charles's cold noncommunication. On the other hand she felt guilty just standing silently; she felt she was shirking her duty to entertain. As the silence stretched longer, animosity, then anger surfaced. Finally she said, "You seem displeased, sir. Has something distressed you?"

Charles impassively looked down his nose at her. "I am, quite simply, disappointed."

"Did the reception not meet your expectations?" she asked disingenuously.

"The gathering was all anyone could wish."

Charles did not seem disposed to speak further without prodding.

"Then someone has distressed you?" she said brightly.

"You have distressed me, Miss Dalrymple," said Charles flatly. His expression was devoid of emotion.

"I, sir?" said Chastity. "Surely you are not serious."

"If there has been a deficiency of seriousness, Miss Dalrymple, I fear I must lay that lack at your feet."

"I do not know, cannot imagine, what you are speaking of."

In a calm voice, and with controlled features, Charles said, "I believed we were progressing toward an understanding. Nothing in your behavior discouraged such a belief. Nothing, that is, until this afternoon, when you made it quite clear your affections have been bestowed upon a party other than myself." He paused, but continued before Chastity could speak. "It is true I had some intimation of your interests once before, when you chose to seclude yourself with a certain individual—I am speaking, of course, of the ball last week—but hope dies hard, and since that time you have shown me what I considered to be signs of favor. I am a fool for accepting at face value behavior that was mere... flirtation."

Chastity was dumbfounded. The speech that Charles had just made was, with the exception of a few examples, almost word for word exactly what she would have said to him if she had the courage to be open. Then she became angry. The priggish insolence of the man! He had bestowed a few charged looks on her, dropped a few innuendoes and insubstantial hints and had assumed she would seize these airy tokens as though they had been the most explicit declarations. These past few weeks she had been made almost ill by an inability to understand Charles's motives, and now he was accusing her of actions that, she would swear, he was guilty of committing. She continued to stand by his side, her hand on his arm, but her face was bright red. She took several deep breaths, but these did not dispel her anger. She was, she supposed, to walk the world with downcast eyes because of a few meaningful glances tossed like scraps across a drawing room or a carriage. The unfairness of Charles's remark, and the self-righteousness with which he made it combined to overcome her self-control. "Flirtation, sir?" she said coldly. "You accuse me of flirting with you, of leading you on? I have never once surpassed the boundaries of polite interest, never once have I been forward with you. My behavior toward you has been a return of yours toward me—I have only responded to your words, manner and attitude; I have initiated none of my own. That you now accuse me of flirtation bespeaks an indelicacy that I am shocked to discover."

Charles had grown white. "It was apparent, Miss Dalrymple, to all the world that my interest in you was beyond the ordinary. That you choose to ignore that interest and bestow—publicly—your attentions on another..."

"Apparent to whom, sir? Not to me. Your ardor has been most cleverly disguised, I assure you." She removed her hand from his arm. She was quite flushed and breathing rapidly. "How dare you accuse me of bestowing public attentions on someone? What kind of behavior do you think me capable of?"

"The whole reception saw the look you gave to Count Orlanov. Or, I should say, the looks—not once, but twice did you favor that gentleman with what can only be called encouragement. I say twice. Perhaps there were other exchanges between you that escaped me."

Like some twig caught in an eddy, Chastity was being twirled and turned and swept along. The more Charles talked the falser grew his picture of her, and the more difficult she found it to impose reality. The vanity of the man was overwhelming! That he should force her to justify herself was testimony to its strength. "I merely happened to glance in the direction where Count Orlanov was standing. I would hardly call that an encouraging gesture."

"Glance, Miss Dalrymple? What I saw—and what everyone near you saw—were quite extended exchanges, studies one might say, between you and the gentleman."

"This is preposterous, sir. You have built an accusation of the basest sort on the strength of two glances."

Charles remained calm and white. "What is preposterous is my self-deception. I thought you were amenable to my attentions. I did not suspect that your heart belonged to another." He spoke with quiet dignity, pained but noble. Chastity found his stance insufferable, but she could not continue trying to alter it without actually pleading her case, a step she refused to take. She stood at a slight distance from him and stared stonily out the large door at nothing.

This was how Lady Trentower found them as she bustled down the stairs. "Very well, we may leave," she said commandingly. "Has the coach been summoned?"

"Yes, ma'am," said Charles tightly. Without another word he stepped through the doorway just as his carriage pulled up to the steps. Lady Trentower went after him, followed by Chastity. Charles handed both women into the carriage with a stony face. Then he announced, "I shall stay a while longer. You will forgive me for not accompanying you." He shut the door and signaled the driver to whip up the horses.

Lady Trentower was incensed. "What kind of behavior is that, pray tell? Has the man taken leave of his senses?" She looked back, trying to see what had become of their escort. Seeing nothing she said to Chastity, "Ah-hah! No doubt he has had a spat with Lady Grasset. A lovers' quarrel. Whenever did it happen, I wonder?" Pleased with this explanation, she settled back against the cushions. Chastity steadfastly stared out the window.

Chapter Nine

The following day Chastity was still reeling from Charles's display of pique. In her imagination she studied the scene from every angle, trying to assess her own responsibility. The first harvest of her examination was guilt and self-doubt; was it possible that she had led Charles on, that she was so little mistress of her own effect on others that she had indeed been flirting? This was short-lived, however, and soon replaced with injured pride; how could the man be so presumptuous as to accuse her of flighty, irresponsible behavior? She kept coming back to the realization that, if she had had the courage, she would have accused Charles of doing to her exactly what he insisted she had done to him.

Underlying his rancor, she decided, was not a broken heart but wounded vanity. He could no doubt have sustained his imagined rejection if it had been discreetly proffered; what set him into a fit was that he thought she had *publicly* preferred another to him.

She wondered, then, with a surmise as unwanted as an icy draft, whether there was some substance to Charles's accusations. Just what did her two long, wordless communications with Count Orlanov mean? Why had she allowed herself to stand as if mesmerized with her eyes locked to his? After as close an inspection of her behavior as she was able to make, she still did not know. Was she, she wondered, leading Count Orlanov on? She shook her head. She neither planned nor schemed behavior toward that man; she was constantly surprised at her reaction to him. She truly did not know what to make of him, and Lady Grasset's revelation only served to further confuse her. On the one hand he had been clearly wrong to take money for such a shady service; on the other, as Lady Grasset so helpfully pointed out, he had acquitted himself in his role of cavalier with the utmost honesty and tact. Surely the one fact canceled out the other? But the count's behavior was not what was ultimately confusing her; it was her own that was mystifying.

Regardless of what she had or had not done, however, she kept coming back to the outright presumptuousness on which Charles's lofty denouncement had been based. He had assumed she was completely at his disposal because he had deigned to bestow a few (very few, she thought bitterly) suggestive looks and words on her. When she had not understood the import of his behavior, he had been insulted. Really, the man was appallingly arrogant.

Yet she could not subdue the anger toward herself for not having correctly interpreted those subtle signs of preference. If only she had more assurance, she told herself, she could have—*would* have—responded in such a way as to make it clear Charles's attentions fell into a favorable climate. She shrugged, sighed and began once more to work her way through the maze of missed opportunities, misunderstandings and confused motives.

Lady Trentower was no help. She started the day with a gleeful assumption that Charles and Lady Grasset had probably made up their little differences during the reception, and that now there would be a real scandal. "Mark my words," she said, all but smacking her lips, "after a lovers' quarrel both will feel obliged to go even further. It would not surprise me if they were to be married. That would be ruinous for Charles," she added with relish. "The woman may be a friend of a Grand Duchess—from *Russia*—but she is still a former streetsinger."

"And your sister-in-law," responded Chastity snidely.

It was the tone of voice as well as the remark that made Lady Trentower glare. "What has gotten into you? You are turning into a very ill-tempered woman. You should watch this tendency in yourself, for nothing puts a man off more quickly than shrewish behavior. Even ugliness is not such a deterrent as that."

"I am not devoting my life to the encouragement of male attention," said Chastity grimly.

"I believe, miss, that if that is the case, you should revise your priorities. A twenty-seven-year-old woman must bring considerably more concentration to the catching of a husband than a seventeen-year-old."

"I am weary of hearing your opinion on this subject," said Chastity.

Lady Trentower, in spite of her niece's recent snappishness, was not accustomed to reprimands.

She was shocked beyond rebuttal. "I wonder," she said, her eyes wide, "whether you are quite well."

"I am," said Chastity. She sullenly refused to meet her aunt's regard.

Lady Trentower continued to stare at her as if to ferret out the core of her behavior. She was baffled. "Well," she said finally, "I cannot quite believe that. We are to go to Lady Holland's to take tea, but frankly I hesitate to encourage you to go into society in this present state."

Chastity rose and stood before her aunt. "I have no wish to go to Lady Holland's, or anywhere else, today. Please make my excuses, if that is necessary." She started to leave the room, then looked back at her aunt. "I hope you have a pleasant outing," she said perfunctorily. She went to her room, leaving Lady Trentower most annoyed.

Two hours later Chastity was informed Count Orlanov had called and was waiting below. Upon inquiry she learned that Lady Trentower had gone to Lady Holland's, so if she was to receive the count, she would have to do so alone. She hesitated while the footman awaited her answer. Then, with a thrust of her chin, she sent word she would descend shortly.

As soon as the footman left she raced to the mirror. She thought she looked haggard. She pinched her cheeks and compressed her lips, bringing the color up. Savagely she brushed her hair until it glistened. Her blue percale dress was one of the newest she owned, so she could not improve upon that. She tossed her head this way and that, keeping her eye fixed on the mirror to judge which angles were most flattering. After a few minutes she sighed, looked straight at her reflection, then left the room.

Count Orlanov was near the fireplace, holding on his left arm his casque with its scarlet cockade. Though he appeared to stand as straight as it was humanly possible for a body to stand, he stiffened even more when she appeared at the door and bowed from the waist. Then he strode toward her, meeting her in the center of the room. He took her hand and bent over it, brushing it with moustache and lips. Chastity's stomach lurched.

"Sir," she said, "this is a pleasure."

"Pleasure is too weak a word. Even I with my poor English realize that. This is ecstasy."

"Won't you take a seat," said Chastity, wondering whether she had been imprudent to meet the man alone.

"Whatever you direct, that I shall do."

She motioned to a small chair, and took one herself at a distance. "Well," she said with a bright smile, "the Grand Duchess's reception was a great success in spite of such very inclement weather."

"For me the success of the day consisted of your presence."

"I hope the Grand Duchess was not too fatigued at the end of the day?"

"I did not notice. I withdrew to savor my memories of you."

"It seemed to me and my aunt every notable in London was present."

"I saw only one presence. You."

Chastity rose. "Sir, I cannot continue to remain with you if you persist in making such inflammatory statements."

Count Orlanov stood also. "I know that you are

trying to be polite, trying to lead the conversation down genteel paths. I wish I had enough self-control to follow you. But I cannot. When I am with you I must express my feelings for you or I shall strangle. Forgive me. I cannot do otherwise."

"You would do well to learn to curb your feelings, sir. I... I am not offended, but I am confused. I have not the experience of such gallant conversation."

"That is one more jewel that adorns you. Or rather, one more facet of the priceless, the flawless, gem that you are."

"I wonder, sir, whether it is wise to be so extravagant with words."

"Words! They cannot begin to convey the depths of my feelings for you. My words are like the tiny flames that dance along the rim of a volcano before it erupts. Just as those flames are the weakest sort of omen of what is to follow, my words are the poorest representation of the strength of my feelings for you."

Chastity trembled slightly, and took her seat again. "You make it..." she began, but had to clear her throat. "You make it very difficult for me to talk to you, sir."

He remained standing, looking fiercely at her. "Then let us cease talking," he said. Chastity, alarmed, shrank. He did not move toward her, but said, "Now you know all there is to know about me. Lady Grasset has implied that she had imparted to you the source of my wealth. I have nothing to hide. You know my past." His blue eyes glistened and his blond curls and moustache gleamed. "You also have control of my future. One word from you and you can exalt me. Another word and you can crush me. You can transport me with a yes. You can smash me with a no. Will you marry me?"

"Sir, I..."

He raised his hand. "I know I have to seek out your father. I intend to do so. But I cannot wait a moment longer to hear from you that you accept my homage, my heart, my soul. I know I am asking you to go against your conventions. I am a brute. Forgive me. But tell me that I do not hope in vain."

"Sir, I am quite sensible to the honor you do me. I am overwhelmed, though, by the intensity of your expression. I cannot..."

"Do not say you cannot accept," said Count Orlanov, looking at her with so much concentration she felt again she was being mesmerized. "To one as delicate as you, to one as unused as you are to rough male attentions, I realize that my suit must seem barbaric. Make an allowance for my passion."

"I assure you, sir, that I am not the delicate creature you seem to think. Not at all. But on the other hand, I do not know how to respond to your so very strong ardor. It is quite fearful..."

"The last thing I wish to do is to frighten you. I am not one of those men who likes a cowering female."

"That, of course, is very heartening..." began Chastity lamely, then stopped. She could think of nothing to say because she did not know what she felt. As always the sight of Count Orlanov was exhilarating; the man was simply superb. But he was so strange, so different from other men she had known, and his fierceness was unlike any behavior she had ever encountered. She was attracted to him and, at the same time, wary of the attraction. Pulled as she was in these two directions, she could not devise any statement that seemed an adequate response to the count's declaration and, at the same time, did not commit her to a course of action she might ultimately find obnoxious. She could not say yes; she was loathe to say no. She said nothing at all.

"You hesitate," said Count Orlanov. "You are wondering about your future with me. We will live where you like. We can return to Saint Petersburg, or we can stay in London. It is all one to me with you by my side."

Chastity summoned dignity to cloak her confusion. She stood. "Sir, I assure you that my place of abode with the man of my choice is of little importance to me. At the same time I am touched—more than touched, shaken—by your willingness to mold your own life better to comply with mine. But I cannot answer you. I must think."

"Do not think. Feel. If you hearkened to your feelings you would not hesitate. You would leave with me this minute."

Chastity took a step backward in alarm. "That, of course, would be impossible, sir," she said. "Even if I were to accept now, there must be time to make suitable arrangements, draw up proper documents."

"I know that. I am not a foolish, reckless man as a rule. My judgment has been distorted by the fear that you will bestow your hand on another." Count Orlanov, his expression still fiercely concentrated, bowed, causing the scarlet cockade to bob at his side. "You must think. Of course you must think. It takes all my self-command to withdraw from your presence while you do so. But I shall leave now, though it pains me." He advanced a few steps toward her, but stopped before greatly diminishing the distance between them. "This has been our first time together alone. Already I treasure and enshrine these moments, though they were all too brief." He bowed again and strode out the door.

Chastity stood looking after him transfixed. She could not summon the strength to move for several moments; then she breathed deeply, gulping air as though she had run a long distance, and collapsed on the nearest gilt chair. She put her hand to her brow, which felt feverish. Shaking her head slightly, she tried to invigorate her intelligence, but she could not impose order on her thoughts. She had always said she yearned for a man of dash. Heaven only knows Count Orlanov qualified; whatever his shortcomings, a lack of dash was not among them. He seemed, when she thought about him, to be everything she could ask for in a suitor; but the reality of the man was so upsetting. As a fantasy he was exactly what she might have dreamed of, had she been given to such wanderings; as flesh and blood he was simply overpowering. Yet, though she was almost certain she could not rise to the heights of emotion where he apparently resided, she could not bring herself to forgo being the object of such lofty passion.

She was still sitting, her forehead in her hand, when Mr. Brockton was announced. Without a moment's hesitation she directed that he be admitted. Mr. Brockton, she thought, would be like a tepid bath, something to calm the nerves. Even if he had arrived to renew his unwanted courtship he would be soothing, for whatever he was capable of saying on the subject would be mild compared to what she had just heard. He was predictable, comfortable.

"Miss Dalrymple," he said as he entered, his ruddy face alight with pleasure, "how delightful to find you at home!" He looked around the room, as though to be sure they were alone, then lowered his voice, as if they were not. "Your servant said there was no one with you, but I scarcely dared to believe it." His eyes twinkled with innocent mischief.

"My aunt is out, and will be sorry to have missed you," said Chastity graciously.

"And I, under most circumstances, would be sorry to miss *her*." He leaned forward confidentially, but without presumption, and said, "But this is most definitely an occurence that is out of the ordinary. Do you realize, Miss Dalrymple, that this is the first time I have had the honor of being with you *en tête à tête*. As the French say."

"I was aware you were speaking French," said Chastity sharply.

"Of course, of course, I forget what a learned woman you are. So delightful to find in one so pretty." He emphasized each syllable as though he were afraid she would miss the compliment.

She nodded with a slight smile. He was like a balm.

Mr. Brockton straightened and erased the playfulness from his expression, ushering in a subject of greater weight. "My original purpose in coming to see you—and your dear aunt—was to say goodbye. I must return to Harrowgate. Business.

Business. Business," he intoned oracularly, shaking his head from side to side. "It is business that tears me from the pleasures of this great city," he lowered his voice, "and from your side."

"I'm sure my aunt will be distressed that she was not here to receive your farewell. I shall convey your message to her."

"That was my *original* purpose, Miss Dalyrmple. But now I find I have the good fortune to see you alone. I shall seize the opportunity. Do not think me forward, Miss Dalrymple, but it cannot have escaped your attention that my interest in you was of a more than passing nature, was, in effect, of a permanent sort."

Until recently this sort of preamble would have made Chastity terminate the conversation or change the subject, or at the very least, fidget. Now she sat calmly regarding Mr. Brockton as he unfurled his declaration. She nodded with a pleasant but impersonal smile as she compared this circuitous statement with Count Orlanov's more direct attack. She was becoming a connoisseur of proposals of marriage.

Interpreting Chastity's bland response favorably, Mr. Brockton cautiously inched ahead. "I know, and esteem, your very worthy family. I am acquainted with your sterling background, and am familiar with your many accomplishments. I am, I can hide the fact no longer, a great admirer of yours!"

"That is very good of you, sir," said Chastity serenely. She realized it would be kinder to deflect Mr. Brockton from his avowals, but the man inspired lassitude, left her drifting along on the gentle current of his platitudes.

Emboldened by her passivity, he pressed harder. "Miss Dalrymple, I must confess that my feeling for you has grown into something rather warmer than admiration." He leaned forward. "It has been my hope this feeling has been reciprocated."

This was the time to stop the conversation, yet Chastity did not. Awash in his sluggish fervor she had no desire to so much as lift a hand to control events. She smiled mysteriously. Mr. Brockton, brightening, interpreted her behavior to his advantage. "I have not hoped in vain!" he said with decorous glee. "I was sure that a kind Providence would answer my prayers!"

Though Chastity had been lulled into an uncritical state, it did not escape her that in all his rambling protestations, Mr. Brockton had not once said either that he loved her or that he wished to marry her. Under those circumstances his cry of triumph was inappropriate. She brought him up rather sharply. "Perhaps, sir, I misunderstand you. What prayers have been answered?"

Mr. Brockton was momentarily thrown off guard; his eyes glazed with incomprehension. Then warily, apologetically he said, "But of course I have been forward. I have taken too much for granted." He reset his features into a serious expression and said, "Miss Dalrymple, life is long when one has to face it without a companion."

Chastity found this tack unexpected, though hardly inspired. She said nothing.

"When two people throw their lots together, however, the burden of progressing toward eternal rest is lightened. Surely you agree?"

He was proving slippery; his circumlocutions were becoming tedious, and something of Chastity's annoyance was evidently stamped on her face, for he hastened to add, "What I mean is that life was meant to be lived in pairs. Man and woman. One without the other is incomplete. That is the Christian view so, of course, it is my view; I am certain it is yours, also."

It occurred to her that Mr. Brockton might be incapable of actually posing the question his discourse ostensibly was leading towards; she took his indirection as a challenge. His proposal became a wily trout to be hooked.

"I am not sure I follow you, sir," she said.

There was sweat on Mr. Brockton's brow. "What I mean, Miss Dalrymple, is that man and woman were destined to be together in a permanent way. I am a man. You are a woman."

"That is indisputable."

"So then, can I hope..."

"Hope what, sir?"

Mr. Brockton looked around the room like one searching an exit. "Miss Dalrymple, will you marry me?"

Chastity felt like slumping into her chair; she was exhausted by the effort of prying out the specific words. She did not let so much as a gleam of satisfaction escape, however, and continued to watch Mr. Brockton with detachment. The effort had cost him heavily. He patted the sweat from his forehead with an immaculate handkerchief, then turned a drained, expectant face toward her.

"I am honored, sir, touched. I appreciate your attention more than I can say. However, I cannot accept your most kind offer...at the present time." The qualification slipped out almost involuntarily. It was not a conscious cruelty on her part, a device to keep Mr. Brockton dangling. Rather, and she did not understand this until later, when she was alone, she had inserted the phrase as a safeguard; she had not the courage to dismiss Mr. Brockton outright. For all her vaunted fastidiousness, she found, now that she had become seriously engaged in the acquisition of a husband, that she could not bring herself to make an irrevocable refusal until she was assured there was something definite to take its place. She now had two proposals. She intended to weigh them both.

Mr. Brockton was not aware of the reasons for her hesitation. He seized a more sanguine explanation. "I understand," he said gravely, "that before taking such a step you must seek advice, ask permission, think and pray for guidance." Solemnly he rose. "I am not precipitate, Miss Dalrymple, nor impatient. I am aware that you, also, are a careful, thoughtful, woman. Your caution is an additional attraction for me. This display of it increases my most fervent hope that your answer will be yes."

Chastity found his characterization of her distasteful. He made her sound exactly like himself, she thought. She held her hand to him in a dismissive gesture. "Sir, you are very kind," she said flatly.

He bent over her hand, keeping a good foot of space between it and his lips. "I leave for Harrowgate this afternoon. Needless to say these next few days will be fraught with suspense for me. I shall live on hope, Miss Dalrymple, hope."

Chastity gave him the smallest of smiles, and

did not return the pressure of his hand. "I am flattered, sir."

Mr. Brockton dropped her hand and said, "May I seek your answer in a week's time?"

With a barely perceptible nod she acquiesced, and he, after a brief but ardent look directly into her eyes, withdrew.

Chastity was far from feeling victorious; on the contrary, she felt rather shabby. Though she had fled Mr. Brockton's courtship for almost a year, she had suddenly been compelled to wrest from him a proposal. Furthermore she had been required to solicit it with more energy than was, in her view, ladylike. She had almost schemed to extract the prized words from the poor man's mouth. Pursuit of a husband could indeed be hard work.

The admission did not make her happy, nor did it lead her to lower her guard in her dealings with her aunt. When Lady Trentower returned from the afternoon with Lady Holland, Chastity was fully determined to keep the two proposals secret. She could not say exactly why; what she did know was that the less Lady Trentower was informed of her affairs, the safer she would feel.

Lady Trentower did not pry into her niece's activities during her absence, because she could not imagine anything worthwhile taking place in a vicinity devoid of her own presence. She assumed that since she had not been at home during the afternoon, Chastity had entered into a state of suspended animation from which she emerged only after her aunt's return.

"There was such a press at Lady Holland's," she began as she entered the drawing room where

Chastity still pensively sat. "It seems all of England is in London now. I suppose because of that Russian. No matter the reason, the crowd was most interesting." She looked at Chastity critically. "You are feeling better, I hope? A pity your indisposition kept you from this afternoon's gathering. You would have been most fascinated by the goings on of a certain pair." Lady Trentower was being arch.

"I feel quite well, as I have all day," said Chastity in the same spirit of contrariness that had marked her intercourse with her aunt that morning.

Lady Trentower decided to avoid another clash. "Well," she said noncommittally. Then, "You should have seen how a certain gentleman hovered around a certain woman. They spent so much time together that it was almost a scandal. It will be one yet." She smiled in anticipation.

"Are you speaking of Mr. Techett and Lady Grasset?" said Chastity calmly.

"I am. And, I daresay, I am not the only one to be speaking of them. I am quite sure they will go away together to Oxford—and that will be the seal on the scandal."

Chastity silently admitted her distress. What she could not admit, because she was not certain, was whether she was jealous that Charles Techett was publicly creating a liaison with Lady Grasset, or was envious that Lady Grasset was able to attract him in spite of her obvious shortcomings, both physical and social.

Lady Trentower talked on. "They went straight to each other as soon as she arrived, took their tea off to a corner, and there they sat for at least a half hour. Then he left and she, of course, made her usual show of greeting all the notables present in most familiar and vulgar terms." Lady Trentower's censures of her sister-in-law were more ritual than heartfelt at this point. Gone was the original venom of her denunciations, though it had hardly been replaced with respect or affection. "Within the week there'll be a scandal!"

Chastity said nothing but, in consolation, hugged her two proposals of marriage to her bosom.

Chapter Ten

As happened not infrequently, Lady Trentower's prediction was incorrect. Not only did Charles Techett not go to Oxford, neither did Lady Grasset. Instead, on the very next day she paid a visit to her dear sister and niece.

"Whatever can the woman want at this hour?" asked Lady Trentower peevishly, but with genuine curiosity, as she was told at breakfast that Lady Grasset had arrived. Chastity also sat up in anticipation.

Lady Grasset rustled into the room, her huge face dimpled with a smile, her eyes glistening with goodwill. "Dear sister and niece! Dare I say my dear family? Indeed I do, for it is so." She pecked Lady Trentower on the cheek, which made the old woman's eyes widen, then paid Chastity the same compliment. "No doubt you think I've lost my reason to be about at such an hour, but there is not enough time to accomplish at conventional hours what I must get done today." She casually took a seat at the table. "Besides, I wanted you both to be the first to know my news."

With sinking heart, Chastity was as certain of Lady Grasset's news as if she had read it in one of the morning gazettes: Charles Techett was going to marry her. Steeling herself, she donned a pleasant smile and a politely inquisitive expression. Lady Trentower, who had arrived at the same conclusion, watched her sister-in-law avidly, crouched like a cat before a mousehole.

"My news will not be very surprising to you," said Lady Grasset, trilling her words in her good spirits, "but it will, I flatter myself to think, cause some little sadness."

Chastity controlled her start; was, she wondered, Lady Grasset being vicious? Had she come to crow about her victory, and Chastity's loss? Though she did not particularly like the woman, at least she had never before now thought her vindictive. Lady Trentower, also, had been nonplussed by Lady Grasset's reference to sadness; she had narrowed her eyes in which an unwonted confusion appeared.

"But," Lady Grasset continued, "I wish to discourage any tears you may have with the reminder that I am absolutely delighted to be undertaking this task." She smiled winsomely. "There's always the possibility I shall return."

"Of what are you speaking," asked Lady Trentower, made restive by perplexity.

"Of my departure. I leave tomorrow."

"Alone?" asked Chastity.

"It is possible I shall have a traveling companion," said Lady Grasset.

"This is very sudden," said Lady Trentower, unable to decide whether to be annoyed at the news.

Lady Grasset shrugged prettily. "The Grand Duchess desires that I prepare the way in Vienna. She now feels she has made a sufficient number of acquaintances here, so she can dispense with my services as her English expert. I shall now become her Austrian expert." She laughed gaily.

Lady Trentower studied her suspiciously. "This is a very strange development," she said.

"Not really. That is, there is nothing strange in it if you know the Grand Duchess, and know me." Lady Grasset thoughtfully flicked a crumb from the tablecloth.

"You mean," said Lady Trentower scornfully, "she can just send you off like this, without any warning."

With the same ingratiating charm she had always lavished on her sister-in-law, Lady Grasset smiled, only this time there was a barely perceptible undercurrent of resistance, a hint that Lady Trentower might go too far. "I am her friend, and when one is a friend to royalty, the usual laws of friendship do not apply. It is of necessity one-sided. The Grand Duchess has the right to exact a great deal of my time and devotion in exchange for her patronage. That is a lesson your brother taught me." Her voice was reasonable, almost condescending.

Lady Trentower stiffened. "I have had, I assure you, sufficient experience with royalty to know how to comport myself in its presence. I am speaking, of course, of *English* royalty."

Lady Grasset was not put off by this show of ire. "I daresay that the intensity of my relationship with the Grand Duchess is greater than what you have known, and it is this fact, and not nationality, which accounts for our dissimilar experiences."

"I can assure you that my connection to royalty

has been as intense as I—or anyone—could wish." Lady Trentower was huffy, and on the defensive.

Instead of acquiescing as she had always done, Lady Grasset offered a good-natured smile spiced with the merest suspicion of sarcasm.

Slight as it was, the hint of derision was too much for Lady Trentower, coming from such a source. She rose imperiously. "I shall withdraw to dress," she said with chilly dignity. "That is my usual custom at this hour, and the custom of my friends, none of whom would dream of going into society before noon." She advanced aloofly to Lady Grasset. "Farewell. Your visit to these shores has proved most interesting." She gingerly extended two fingers.

With a laugh that sounded genuinely amused, Lady Grasset jumped to her feet, moving with alarming agility for one so large. She avoided the two fingers pointing at her waist and clasped the older woman by the shoulders. Then she placed a resounding kiss on both cheeks. "Farewell, dearest sister," she said. "How I shall miss you. Of course we must correspond."

Lady Trentower pulled out of her embrace with the look of one who has been assaulted. She stared an instant at Lady Grasset, her mouth working; then, apparently unable to find proper words to express her outrage at this unwarranted show of affection, she stalked from the room.

Looking highly pleased, Lady Grasset returned to her seat. Chastity had witnessed the charade with a certain satisfaction at her aunt's discomfort. Now, however, she felt uneasy at being alone with the woman who was capable of such impetuosity. "So, you will be leaving London," she said blandly. "So many friends will miss you."

"That's kind of you to say but, of course, it's not true," said Lady Grasset offhandedly. "I have very few friends in London. One or two at the most."

"On the contrary," said Chastity, taken aback, "you have met everyone, and are received everywhere."

"I'm received as the representative of the Grand Duchess. She could send a poodle on the same rounds and it would garner as much attention and honor as I have." Lady Grasset was free of rancor. She smiled. "It would be unthinkable for me to stay in London once the Grand Duchess leaves. I should be ostracized the minute she departed, not only because of my background, but because as soon as the story of my relations with Count Orlanov and my husband is revealed I shall be considered scandalous."

"I can assure you your secret is safe with me," said Chastity primly, as though she had been accused of spreading the tale.

Lady Grasset laughed. "I'm sure. Only, my secret, as you call it, is not safe with *me*. I could never bear to be silent about my past. It is not in my nature to be silent about anything. I have, as I told you, an urge toward revelation. One day I should find myself telling the story in all its details to... let us say... Lady Trentower." She laughed again. "Now, can you imagine my fate in that quarter once I have recounted how my husband bought for me a paramour?"

Chastity could imagine all too well the outcome of such a conversation. Even she, who prided herself on her broadness of view, inwardly cringed as

Lady Grasset specified the nature of her ties to Count Orlanov. At the same time she was nervously gratified that the woman seemed to be veering toward another of her bouts of total honesty, for a question was rankling.

"You said you might have a traveling companion," she began timidly.

"That is true," said Lady Grasset, regarding her with amusement.

"I suppose that...uh...a certain gentleman is planning to join you?"

Lady Grasset's peal of laughter brought a flush to Chastity's face. "A certain gentleman?" she said teasingly.

With an almost stern dignity, Chastity asked, "Is Mr. Techett joining you?"

The question brought a blank look of surprise to Lady Grasset's eyes. "Mr. Techett? For heaven's sake, what has given you that idea?"

"I...I just thought..." Chastity paused in confusion. What had given her the idea had been her aunt's insistence that there was a scandal brewing between the two.

"How droll. The mere thought of going off with Charles is enough to render me quite giddy."

This dismissal of Charles Techett had in it something contemptuous, and Chastity was offended. "I understood," she said coldly, "that you and he had been seen together quite frequently."

"We have met in public places, and we always enjoy exchanging views. Has there been a romantic interpretation of such meetings?" She laughed again. "Poor Charles would be beside himself if he knew gossip of this sort was afoot."

Chastity could not quite believe this lighthearted dismissal of a situation she was certain had greater weight than Lady Grasset seemed willing to assign to it. She could not resist probing further, trying to elicit details. "But you were seen together for half an hour yesterday...at Lady Holland's, I am told."

Lady Grasset's brows shot up quizzically as she made an effort to remember. "Half an hour? As long as that? Who, I wonder, was keeping count of the minutes?" She smiled ironically. "It is true we did have quite a chat yesterday. I told him of my plans for departure, and we discussed Vienna, which he knows." She shook her head ruefully, as she kept her eyes fixed on Chastity. "That is all. It was a very innocent half hour, I assure you."

"Then," said Chastity almost to herself, "Mr. Techett will not be joining you."

"Certainly not. When I referred to a possible traveling companion I thought surely you would understand I was talking about Peter. It is he who might join me, if he does not receive a favorable answer from you." Lady Grasset raised her hand as Chastity began to blush. "He did not tell me this. All he has said to me is that he has offered you his life—those were his words—and that he is waiting for you to accept it. I merely assume that if you refuse to take Peter's life, he will find Vienna more congenial than London." She made a wryly amused face, as though she were sharing a joke about some mutual acquaintance's eccentricities.

"I see," said Chastity.

"Now, in the light of your interest in Charles's whereabouts, I assume I shall be joined by Peter."

Chastity reflexively opened her mouth to deny

the statement, then stopped. She looked boldly at Lady Grasset who was watching her with amusement, and said, "Mr. Techett does not return my interest. Or rather, he said he was at one time ready to offer his hand—at least that was my understanding—but then he accused me of flirting with Count Orlanov and withdrew it."

"Withdrew the hand he had not yet offered?" said Lady Grasset, laughing. "That sounds very much like Charles."

Chastity made a hopeless gesture, signifying confusion and unhappiness. "I did not understand clearly his objections to my behavior."

Lady Grasset nodded, as though she understood everything. "That does not surprise me. Charles is a master at working others into disadvantageous positions; or, at the very least, of convincing them that such is the case."

"You seem to know him very well," said Chastity contentiously.

Lady Grasset ceased smiling and looked thoughtful. "I once offended you by stating that Charles Techett would not be a good match for you. At the risk of incurring your displeasure, I must revive that subject." She looked at Chastity with theatrical sadness. "Charles is undeniably handsome, he is polished. He has dash," her eyes glinted with a brief flick of amusement, "and he is financially secure, so he no longer needs to marry for money. All these qualities are desirable in a spouse, no doubt. But Charles has other traits. He is a cold, vain man, easily thrust into jealousy—why, he is even jealous of Peter, who hardly knows he exists."

Chastity regarded her with hostility. "I thought he was your friend."

"He is very much my friend. These tendencies in a friend are quite supportable. In a husband they are obstacles to a happy marriage."

"By your own admission you have both changed since ten or so years ago. Perhaps you no longer know him as well as you think."

Lady Grasset slowly shook her head from side to side. "We have not so much changed as become exaggerated. What were only traces, hints, possibilities, over a decade ago, now have developed into full blown characteristics. My unfortunate frankness, for example, was not nearly so severe then as now. Charles's pride, by the same token, has taken on weight over the years. I know Charles very well, and he knows me. So well that we could never again be lovers."

"Was there a possibility... were you..." Chastity could not leap into the unconfined pasture of Lady Grasset's candidness, and had to settle for allusions.

"I thought there might be a possibility of our resuming—or renewing—our relationship," said Lady Grasset. "It was only human to want to revive the first and greatest love of my life. I have no idea what fantasies Charles entertained on the subject. Five minutes together quite convinced us both there was nothing left of our affair but memory. We settled into friendship." She smiled. "As a friend, as I said, he is quite delightful. As a husband—particularly for you—he would be a disaster."

"Why do you insist upon my unsuitability? What right have you to pass judgment on me?"

"I assure you," said Lady Grasset placatingly, "that no criticism of you is intended. I am simply bringing my experience to bear on the situation, and hope you will allow me to share it with you."

"You may very well know Mr. Techett. You do not know me."

"I don't know you as well as I should like, of course, but I have observed you quite enough to have formed an opinion. I realize I am subject to error, but then, I have seen more of the world than you, so perhaps you will be forbearing enough to let me voice my impressions." She spoke reasonably, quietly. Chastity would have felt petty if she had followed her inclination to stop the discussion. She compromised by keeping a guarded, stony expression, which did not deter Lady Grasset. "I believe you expect a great deal from matrimony and from your husband. I think, in fact, that you have a very romantic notion of what marriage is. Charles will never fill your needs. He will be, at best, a part-time husband, indifferent to you once he finds he has completely captured your affections. It is his nature to strive, to ingratiate, but not to rest content with his conquests. Once he learns that you are his without reservation, he will quite simply lose interest in you. His pride, or vanity, I'm not sure which, will keep pushing him toward new conquests. I assure you I know of what I speak."

"Did he lose interest in you?" asked Chastity sarcastically.

Lady Grasset shook her head. "What we had together was an infatuation, and we were both much younger and inexperienced. He did not lose interest, because circumstances separated us—

circumstances dictated by his own very clear-headed assessment of his needs. When he decided he must marry an heiress he put me aside (though, to do him justice, he suffered every bit as much as me, and did provide for me by furnishing his own godfather to be my husband). This was not because he had lost interest in me, but because everyone—society, his family, his friends—all were urging marriage on him." She paused thoughtfully. "However, had we remained together any longer I can assure you he would have become bored with me."

"Are you sure you are not speaking of him in bitterness? He did send you away." Chastity tried to keep the edge of spite out of her voice but failed.

Lady Grasset was not annoyed. She gently shook her head and said, "He sent me away, true, but he was acting at the behest of every social pressure that existed at the time. No, I am not bitter against him. I like him. He is, as I told you, my friend. But that does not mean he would be a good husband for you. Tell me," she said suddenly, "why will you not consider Mr. Brockton?"

Chastity was brought up sharply. In a sense she *was* considering Mr. Brockton, since she had not refused his proposal, and she glanced quickly at Lady Grasset to see whether her question was based on awareness of this fact. But her expression bore no sign of secret knowledge. "I simply do not care for him," she said stiffly.

Shaking her head, Lady Grasset made a rueful clicking of her tongue. "He would make a perfect husband for you. He will never grow tired of his wife, but remain constantly in awe of her, perpetually grateful to her for having chosen him. He is kind. He is wealthy. He is...perfect."

Chastity took a deep breath. "No doubt Mr. Brockton is all that you say. But I do not wish to marry him, not because of what he is or is not, but because of what he would make of me. I would be as dull as he after a few years." This reason just slipped out, and surprised Chastity more than it did Lady Grasset. After she had said it, however, she realized it was the truth. She feared Mr. Brockton's power to reduce her to a replica of himself.

Lady Grasset cocked an eyebrow and pursed her lips as she pondered the remark. After a pause, she said, "Well, then, if you are looking for a husband who will make a more interesting you, it is incontestable that either Peter or Charles are to be recommended. Both would cause you to struggle, would create unhappiness—Peter through incomprehension of your needs, and Charles through indifference to them. But of course we must pay for our transformations with pain; such things do not happen for nothing. I certainly know that, for my husband changed me completely." She nodded with a wry smile. "Well, well. I have nothing more to say. So you will marry Charles."

"He has not asked me," said Chastity shortly. She was annoyed at the woman's forecast, given with such assurance. She would have liked, in some way, to get the better of Lady Grasset, to show her up, to belittle her prognostications. She did not dare, for she did not feel competent to challenge the assessments. She did, however, display an unfriendly expression.

Lady Grasset brushed aside her disclaimer. "I

think he will ask you soon enough. He wants to remarry and soon. He has political ambitions, and feels the need of what he calls a 'safe' wife." She smiled. "Yesterday, at Lady Holland's we talked about more than Vienna, I must confess."

Though she knew it was undignified, Chastity could not stop herself from asking, "Did he mention me?"

Lady Grasset shook her head. "No, he did not. He mentioned several other women, but very pointedly passed over your name. That is what makes me certain he is determined to woo and win you. He is very secretive. But you will find all that out soon enough."

Chastity was divided between feeling grateful to Lady Grasset for bearing this opinion, and anger at her omniscience. Lady Grasset continued, "No doubt he will declare himself once he is certain he will be accepted. His vanity is such that he could never dare risk a refusal."

"But," Chastity could not help asking, "how shall he know?"

Lady Grasset laughed. "I suspect you'll tell him. In one way or another." She looked around her. "I must be going. I have to make the rounds to say goodbye to all my new friends—soon to be my former friends." She laughed again. "I am looking forward to Vienna. It will be very heady. They say the congress there will be the greatest the world has ever known. Perhaps," she said slyly, "Charles will take you there for your honeymoon." She stood.

Chastity rose also, trying to find a proper attitude. She did not want the leavetaking to be openly hostile since the woman had not, she did not think, been vicious. On the other hand, she felt no warmth toward her, and did not wish to display any effusiveness. Her indecision was swept aside by Lady Grasset who grasped both her shoulders, as she had done to Lady Trentower, and kissed both her cheeks.

"Goodbye, my dear," she said. "I have enjoyed our friendship." With a rustle of yards of black silk she was gone, leaving Chastity, a tentative smile on her lips, standing in the middle of the room.

Chapter Eleven

Later, on the day Lady Grasset said her farewell—and so much else—Chastity asked herself why the woman had been so outspoken. Such involvement in another's affairs was behavior that she, Chastity, was incapable of, and she could not comprehend how a comparative stranger could rush into one's life upsetting conventions. It was true that Lady Grasset had been every bit as open about herself and her own strange past as she had been about Chastity's concerns. Why, Chastity wondered, did she pick me? Surely she was not so open with everyone, or the gossip would have raced through London like a windstorm. Rather than being flattered that there was evidently some quality in her that had struck a responsive chord in her younger aunt, Chastity was disturbed at the idea that possibly she had, in some way, encouraged this unfortunate frankness.

In addition, there were jolting resonances from some of Lady Grasset's disclosures, such as "Charles needs a 'safe' wife..." What was a safe wife? One who would give no trouble, would not be in the way; one who would quite simply be a cipher? This was not the way Chastity wished to see herself, as a patient homebody waiting by the hearth while her husband went about his business. Lady

Grasset had made her sound stodgy, and she could not forgive that.

Chastity met Lady Trentower in the drawing room later in the day. The older woman had reverted to her original position of wholesale censure of her sister-in-law. Now that the rotund Lady Grasset was no longer to be reckoned with in person, Lady Trentower forgot that the woman might have had some redeeming features, and that to be her sister-in-law had, for a few brief moments, actually carried some social advantage. "So she is gone," she said with satisfaction. "I knew she wouldn't be able to last in London. It was inevitable that she would be seen through."

"She has gone at the behest of the Grand Duchess, and not because of any rejection here," Chastity pointed out.

"Nonsense," said Lady Trentower. "The Grand Duchess is just an excuse. I've been thinking, and you can mark my words, the woman is leaving because the best drawing rooms would have been closed to her before long—including this one."

Though this was not at the moment true, Chastity reflected that in all probability it would have been the case if Lady Grasset, as she had emphasized herself, had decided to remain in London.

Lady Trentower smacked her lips. "I knew that she would never last." Then, "I wonder when Charles will join her?"

"He will not join her," said Chastity.

"Don't you believe it. Not for a minute. She said this morning, in my dining room, that she *might* have a traveling companion. Might indeed. She takes me for a child." Lady Trentower looked around her drawing room with a pleased smile.

"As soon as it is known that Charles has joined her he will have to live on the Continent, for he will not be welcome in society here." She nodded several times in anticipation of this happy development.

Just then Charles Techett was announced. Lady Trentower was momentarily discommoded, but recovered immediately. "He has come to say goodbye," she whispered portentously, a second before Charles entered the drawing room.

He did not look like one on the verge of being proscribed. On the contrary, he was as elegantly at ease as he had always been, was as meticulously groomed, and on his face there was no trace of the cold displeasure Chastity had last seen there. He bowed affably to both women.

"Well, Charles," said Lady Trentower, "I am pleased that you can spare me some time. Yesterday, though I *saw* you, I could not tear you away from a certain person's side. You barely nodded in my direction." Her eyes gleamed maliciously.

"I must have been momentarily blinded to have forgone the pleasure of talking to you," said Charles agreeably. "Now, I hope, you will allow me to make up for my loss." He turned to Chastity. "How are you, Miss Dalrymple?" he asked politely with a show of concern. "We were most distressed to have missed you yesterday at Lady Holland's. I hope you have not been ill?"

"Not at all, sir, thank you for your kindness," said Chastity. At first she was not certain how to behave. She wondered whether she should still be haughty as befitted one who has been unjustly accused of public flirting, or whether she should pretend the strange scene had never happened. Then, remembering Lady Grasset's words—that Charles would only propose if he were certain he would not be refused—she fell into a pose of easy goodwill, with whatever prickliness she might have harbored well hidden away. She smiled sweetly.

"I suppose you have heard," said Lady Trentower, squinting in her eagerness for the kill, "that a certain person will be leaving London today?"

"Lady Grasset, you mean?" said Charles with a little moue of regret. "Yes, and society shall be poorer for her loss. I'm sure you will miss her every bit as much as I do."

Lady Trentower's laugh sounded almost like a snort. "I can't say she will leave any large holes in my existence," she said with satisfaction. "But then, of course, I was not given to long *tête à tête*'s with her in public."

"As I was, you're implying," said Charles, laughing. "I understand that my conversation with Lady Grasset yesterday caused some misinterpretation of our friendship."

"Indeed. Misinterpretation, you say? From whom have you heard this?"

"From Lady Grasset herself. I saw her last evening to make my farewells."

"Hmm," said Lady Trentower knowingly, but otherwise held her peace and contented herself with a broad look of skepticism.

Charles appeared not to notice. To Chastity he said, "I suppose you will miss your other aunt, Miss Dalrymple?"

Still smiling pleasantly, Chastity replied, "Certainly I shall. She was most agreeable to me during her brief stay."

"As she was to us all," said Charles. "Ah, well, life is like that. People come and go, and one never gets used to change." He expressed these sentiments in a pleasant, not very aggrieved voice.

"And you, Charles," said Lady Trentower, tired of shilly-shallying, "will you be taking a little trip soon?"

Charles regarded her with amusement. "Are you eager to get rid of me?"

Lady Trentower was not susceptible to teasing, but wanted facts. "Come, come. Answer me outright."

"Why, yes," said Charles pleasantly. He looked directly at Chastity for an instant before adding, "I might take a little jaunt through Kent."

"Kent?" said Lady Trentower blankly. "Kent? What does that mean?"

Chastity regarded him fixedly for a few seconds before dropping her eyes to her lap. Charles answered Lady Trentower, "I fear it means exactly what I have said. Alas, I bear no hidden meanings."

"But why Kent?" persisted Lady Trentower.

"I might have some very personal business there," said Charles smoothly. His eyes met Chastity's again for a significant instant before sliding back to Lady Trentower.

So intent was Lady Trentower on proving that this was some subterfuge, some plot to enable Charles to slip off to Vienna that she remarked none of the play between her niece and visitor. Shrewdly she said, "I suppose you'll be leaving soon?"

"That depends upon developments in the... near future."

"Developments. Hmm. What might they be?" asked Lady Trentower.

Charles shrugged. "I cannot give all my secrets away or you'll no longer find me interesting," he said with a laugh.

Lady Trentower nodded her head several times with great emphasis, as if to say, I told you so. She looked extremely knowing. "Well," she said, "what other news is there?" She appeared to be settling in for the rest of the afternoon, attached to Charles like a barnacle.

Chastity was beside herself with frustration. "Perhaps," she said, "you would care for tea or wine, Mr. Techett?"

Charles nodded affably. "Wine, I think."

Chastity pulled the cord, and when the footman appeared ordered refreshments. She had about her a purposefulness that went unremarked by her aunt, who continued to quiz Charles.

The footman brought the tray with wine and little cakes, and Chastity asked, "Will you have some, ma'am?" to the still chattering Lady Trentower.

"What? Wine? You know I will not. I might take tea a little later, but not now." She returned to Charles, but did not have time to finish the statement she was making, for Chastity had poured a glass of wine and in bearing it toward her aunt, in spite of the protestations, she stumbled and the contents flew down the front of the old woman's dress.

"My heavens, what have you done!" said Lady Trentower as the claret soaked her bosom and dripped with sinister effect into her lap. "Clumsy! How awkward you are!"

"Forgive me, how very foolish of me," said Chastity with the barest show of solicitude, and she made an ineffectual attempt to pat the moisture from the gown.

"Leave it, leave it," said Lady Trentower huffily. "I shall have to change. Really, you should be more careful."

"I'm so dreadfully sorry," said Chastity in the most perfunctory of voices. Calmly, she poured another glass of wine and carefully handed it to Charles, who received it with a wise look. Lady Trentower hastily left the room muttering that she would return, and Chastity took a seat near Charles.

"How very clumsy I am," she murmured penitently.

"On the contrary, Miss Dalrymple, Terpischore herself could not have executed a movement that would have delighted me more."

Chastity smiled shyly. "That is very kind of you, under the circumstances."

"It is only true." His eyes stayed on hers as he said, without any preamble, "I have come today for two reasons. The first is to beg your forgiveness."

"Sir?"

"For the scene I made when we were last together. I was carried away by...never mind. Please do forgive me."

Chastity lowered her eyes. "Of course," she said softly.

There was a long silence as she waited for him to enunciate the second reason. Though he did not lose his air of insouciance, he did hesitate a long while before speaking again. Finally, in a more subdued tone than she had ever heard him use, he said, "I hope you have been aware of my esteem for you during the few weeks we have known each other."

"I had hoped that my own regard had found a positive reception," said Chastity hesitantly.

"If I had known for certain that your opinion of me was favorable, I should not have delayed speaking for so long."

Chastity raised her eyes to his, and waited. Again he was silent for an inordinately long time. She began to be afraid that, like Mr. Brockton, he would be content with half phrases and allusions, and would not pose the question without a great deal of effort on her part. She silently returned her eyes to her lap.

With obvious difficulty Charles said, "I was so unsure of your views of me that I had almost resolved to abandon the pursuit of your hand." Chastity raised her eyes in genteel alarm. "But then last night Lady Grasset assured me that my suit would not be scorned."

This mention of Lady Grasset at such a juncture struck Chastity as being exceedingly ill-timed. She had to suppress a comment to the effect that Lady Grasset was not the arbiter of her, Chastity's, emotional life. She continued to stare silently at her lap.

"I am grateful to her for enlightening me, for if she had not I would have felt it too unlikely that you would consider me. I still realize that I am unworthy of you; but I dare to hope that even with all my shortcomings you will cast a tolerant eye upon my presumption." Charles remained the picture of elegant ease as he professed his lack of qualifications. There was, however, a greater than usual gleam of sincerity in his eye.

"I assure you, sir, that whatever your shortcomings may be, they have been invisible to me."

"How dear you are." He fell silent. Chastity began to fear that Lady Trentower would return before he had unburdened himself of the fateful question. She smiled encouragingly. He returned the smile and moved his chair nearer her. Hesitantly he took her hand. "Will you be my wife?"

"I . . . I am honored."

He looked at her expectantly.

"Yes," she murmured softly, her eyes lowered. He raised her hand and barely brushed it with his lips. She felt a little tremor, whether of desire or satisfaction, she could not have said. It might be, as Lady Grasset had insisted, that Charles Techett was vain, egotistical, proud, and would eventually prove indifferent. At the moment, however, he was exactly what she wanted. Furthermore, even if the inauspicious portrait (painted by a woman he had rejected, whatever the reasons) were accurate, it was of a man who existed before she had entered his life. Who knew what changes she would effect. She lifted her head to look directly into his large black, contented eyes. She was flushed and short of breath.

"Now," he said, "I must indeed make that trip to Kent to meet with your father. Will he be agreeable to my quest, do you think?" His question was formal, and the manner in which it was asked left no doubt that he was as certain of an excellent reception at Grangeford as elsewhere.

"How could he not, when his own daughter's happiness depends upon his assent?" said Chastity softly.

"Dearest," said Charles.

He sat up straight and dropped her hand as the door opened and Lady Trentower entered in a dark blue silk gown. "Well," she said with an expulsion of breath, "I hope to be able to finish the afternoon without changing again." She looked peevishly at Chastity, who was prevented from making any response by the entrance of a footman who announced that Count Orlanov had arrived.

"Count Orlanov?" said Lady Trentower looking at the other two. "He is still in London, then?" Her expression took on more animation as she contemplated having the rivals for Lady Grasset's affection confront each other in her drawing room. "Show him in," she commanded, and then, to Charles, "I do hope this does not distress you?"

"Not at all," said Charles coldly.

Chastity was, for a few seconds, in a quandary. She rose to greet the count.

He entered quickly, carrying his casque under his left arm. He bowed to Lady Trentower, nodded to Charles, and walked to stand in front of Chastity. He looked down into her eyes for a long moment. Then he took her hand, bent over it and she felt his soft warm skin and golden moustache as he lingered there. Quietly she withdrew her hand and said, "Count Orlanov, I am pleased to see you, particularly at this time, because I wish you to be among the first to share my good news." He watched her unblinkingly out of his fierce blue eyes. Chastity continued. "Today, Mr. Techett has done me the honor of asking for my hand in marriage. I have accepted. I am very happy."

Count Orlanov, on the whole, took the news much better than Lady Trentower. He bowed to her again, and then, stepping back, bowed to Charles.

"What? What is that you say? How can that be?" said Lady Trentower. "When did this happen?" She looked from Charles to Chastity, her face contorted with indignation. "Is this some pleasantry? It is not funny."

Chastity allowed the merest hint of arrogance to color her reply, "This is an agreement Mr. Techett and I have reached quite recently."

"I should think so!" said Lady Trentower. She turned accusingly to Charles. "What about..." But even she was not insensitive enough to introduce Lady Grasset's name at such a moment, although her struggle to suppress it was visible.

Count Orlanov went to the table where the wine was standing and poured a glass. "I wish to drink to your happiness," he said to Chastity. He swallowed the contents at a gulp. Then he smashed the glass against the hearth and the shards danced brilliantly across the floor.

"Good heavens, the man has taken leave of his senses!" said Lady Trentower. Chastity and Charles both started, and then stared as Count Orlanov, with no change of expression bowed again and briskly left the room.

"The man is mad," said Lady Trentower. Her sense of order had been as shattered as the glass by the behavior not only of Count Orlanov, but also of Chastity and Charles. She found it impossible to accept news so at odds with her own predictions. She glared at them.

Charles said, "I must be off to prepare for a rapid trip to Kent." He smiled at Lady Trentower, "Now you understand the reason for my voyage."

"Yes," said Lady Trentower icily.

"I know you wish both me and your niece all possible happiness."

"Of course."

Charles took Chastity's hand. "I shall return to London as soon as I can. Every hour from your side will be painful."

"I will be waiting for you," said Chastity softly. With another long look and an affectionate smile, Charles left.

"What about Mr. Brockton?" said Lady Trentower, determined to impose order upon chaos. "I thought he would be the perfect husband for you."

Chastity was beyond vexation. "I shall write Mr. Brockton now, to tell him I shall not marry him," she said quietly. Serenely, and with great dignity, she left her aunt and ascended to her room, where she would write not only to Mr. Brockton, but also to her father and sisters, and tell them the astonishing and unlooked for news. Soon she would be married.

GREAT ADVENTURES IN READING

THE MONA INTERCEPT   14374 $2.75
by Donald Hamilton
A story of the fight for power, life, and love on the treacherous seas.

JEMMA   14375 $2.75
by Beverly Byrne
A glittering Cinderella story set against the background of Lincoln's America, Victoria's England, and Napolean's France.

DEATH FIRES   14376 $1.95
by Ron Faust
The questions of art and life become a matter of life and death on a desolate stretch of the Mexican coast.

PAWN OF THE OMPHALOS   14377 $1.95
by E. C. Tubb
A lone man agrees to gamble his life to obtain the scientific data that might save a planet from destruction.

DADDY'S LITTLE HELPERS   14384 $1.50
by Bil Keane
More laughs with The Family Circus crew.

Buy them at your local bookstore or use this handy coupon for ordering.

COLUMBIA BOOK SERVICE (a CBS Publications Co.)
32275 Mally Road, P.O. Box FB, Madison Heights, MI 48071

Please send me the books I have checked above. Orders for less than 5 books must include 75¢ for the first book and 25¢ for each additional book to cover postage and handling. Orders for 5 books or more postage is FREE. Send check or money order only.

Cost $ _____   Name _____

Sales tax* _____   Address _____

Postage _____   City _____

Total $ _____   State _____ Zip _____

* *The government requires us to collect sales tax in all states except AK, DE, MT, NH and OR.*

This offer expires 1 September 81

NEW FROM FAWCETT CREST

DOMINO by Phyllis A. Whitney	24350	$2.75
CLOSE TO HOME by Ellen Goodman	24351	$2.50
THE DROWNING SEASON by Alice Hoffman	24352	$2.50
OUT OF ORDER by Barbara Raskin	24353	$2.25
A FRIEND OF KAFKA by Isaac Bashevis Singer	24354	$2.50
ALICE by Sandra Wilson	24355	$1.95
MASK OF TREASON by Anne Stevenson	24356	$1.95
POSTMARKED THE STARS by Andre Norton	24357	$2.25

Buy them at your local bookstore or use this handy coupon for ordering.

COLUMBIA BOOK SERVICE (a CBS Publications Co.)
32275 Mally Road, P.O. Box FB, Madison Heights, MI 48071

Please send me the books I have checked above. Orders for less than 5 books must include 75¢ for the first book and 25¢ for each additional book to cover postage and handling. Orders for 5 books or more postage is FREE. Send check or money order only.

Cost $_____ Name _____

Sales tax*_____ Address _____

Postage_____ City _____

Total $_____ State _____ Zip _____

The government requires us to collect sales tax in all states except AK, DE, MT, NH and OR.

This offer expires 1 September 81